Set in Her Ways

Jenny Telfer Chaplin

Jenny Telfer Chaplin

Published by Kinnon Enterprises Ottawa

ISBN: 978-0-9698825-4-1

PROLOGUE

1906

Mrs Bridget Reilly, as she worked around her Gorbals single-end wee palace that morning was trying hard to ignore the early pangs of childbirth. A careworn woman just turned forty and old before her time, her life's experience had already made her something of an expert on the subject of child birth. Ever since the birth, the excruciatingly painful birth of her twin sons, the annual ritual for her had been a miscarriage with the resultant misery, not least of which, the dashing of her hopes for a wee girl.

Aye, she thought, *a wee girl would make sense of these past years of discomfort, misery and stark disappointment.*

At the same time she knew that another reason for her reluctance to send for the local self-styled midwife – apart from the cost involved – was the inborn fear that yet again a miscarriage or worse still, a perfectly-formed baby who lived only a few hours would be the end-result. Laying down her vinegar-soaked cleaning cloth and abandoning all pretence at housework, she instead made herself a mug of hot, sweet tea. Settling back in the master's chair, just as she raised the mug to her lips, a fierce, agonizing pain shot through her body. At the same time, a babbled noise seemed to echo through her head. For a moment, she could almost believe that the sounds were coming from of all things, the pavement in front of her ground floor home.

"Dear God," she said, "As if labour-pains wurnae bad enough in themselves, noo it feels as if this time Ah'm goin aff ma heid as weel."

Again seeking some modicum of comfort from a gulp of tea, she became aware of something else. A frantic rat-a-tat-tat at her door, quickly followed by the entrance of Mrs Mulvaney, her neighbour from across the landing of the common close. Old and asthmatic as she was, for once the ancient crone seemed to be moving with unusual and enviable speed. Without pausing for the habitual and locally accepted greeting of, "It's only me, hen", Mrs Mulvaney, a wild look in her watery eyes, yelled: "Bridie, Bridie – get yer bum outa that chair. Ye and me – we'll need for tae get the hell outa here this very minute. There's been a terrible accident."

By now convinced that she was in the throes of a vividly real nightmare, Bridget shook her head in an effort to clear her thoughts. On seeing this, the older woman grabbed hold of her neighbour's arms and tried physically to wrest her from the armchair. In resisting this, Bridget shrank back with the words: "In the name of all the Saints what's come over ye, Frances? Ah was feeling ill enough before ye started this nonsense – what's got into ye, woman?"

Before Mrs Mulvaney could answer, Bridget happened to glance down at her neighbour's feet. The old woman's moth-eaten sandshoes looked decidedly damp and the ends of her long skirts hung limp about her, almost as if she'd waded her way through a sea of puddles in order to reach her goal.

Catching the look, Frances snapped: "Aye, ma lassie, ye can stare all ye like at ma baffies and ma drookit skirts. Ah had tae slosh ma way across the close for tae get in here. Like Ah say, there's been an accident and any minute now yer house and mine – they're gonnae be flooded out."

Bridget levered herself out of the chair. "Ye mean a burst pipe, out in the street? Uch, we've had that many a time before. Bad enough, Ah'll grant ye, but no disastrous enough to get yerself intae such a paddy. Calm doon, Frances. Anyway, Ah've got other problems of my ain right noo."

The old woman shook off Bridie's would-be calming hand. "Burst pipe be damned. Flooding Ah said. Word on the street is – that Loch Katrine Distillery roon the corner, it's the three big distillery vats, they've only went and burst. The polis himsel telt me tae get the hell oota ma hoose – run like hell, he said, – for there's something like sixty thousand gallons of liquid pourin intae the streets, a tidal wave, he cried it and God help us all, but naethin tae stop it in its path."

As the full import of her neighbour's words dawned on Bridget, she grabbed up her shawl and together the two women bustled out into the street – a street which was by now a river alive with people in all states of dress and undress and slithering, sloshing about in desperately fleeing from their beleaguered homes. As they continued to slither about, trying to keep upright against the force of the surging liquid, Bridget's last thought before she fainted into the arms of a hastily-summoned policeman: Trust me to go into labour on a day like this.

Even with this thought uppermost in her mind neither woman dared mention the fact that Bridget's husband and her two sons worked at the top of the distillery – by all accounts, the very level which had collapsed on to the floors below, causing the massive distillery vats to burst, with the unstoppable outpouring of thousands of gallons of liquid with nowhere else to go other than rampaging through the streets, shops and tenement homes of Glasgow's Gorbals.

Although not a word was uttered as to the feared disastrous fate of the men folk in Bridget Reilly's life, even so the thought kept hammering through her brain as she was helped towards the police station by two burly stalwarts of law and order, closely followed by a concerned Mrs Mulvaney. Above the would-be comforting sounds of: "There, there, hen, it'll no be long noo," in Bridget's own mind, all she could think was: *God alone knows how this day will end ... will Ah be a widow, a new Mother ... or grief-stricken with my two braw laddies gone tae meet their Maker ... and me, alone and bereft, here in the land-o-the-livin with yet anither still-born bairn ... God alone knows how this day will end.*

ONE

1920

As fourteen-year-old Mima Reilly made her way along the early morning city streets to Glasgow's most famous and world-renowned biscuit manufactory, she could feel her spirits dampen with every step she took. While the other young girls in her section of the factory would be alert, bright, and desperate to impart news of the latest church soiree or Band of Hope Lantern lecture and bun fight they had attended with their newest click, Mima alone had no such high hopes. She was all-too-aware that her so-called news, far from being of interest to any captive audience, would do nothing other than disgust them. Even worse, and she'd seen it all before, her tale of woe would immediately produce a crop of wrinkled noses, pursed lips and exaggerated strangled cries of, "That fair gives me the dry boak" together with a grotesque pantomime of noisy retching.

Despite herself, Mima had to grin at the vivid mental image and thought: *Ah suppose in all fairness, there's not another lassie in the whole of Glasgow who could be remotely interested either in the number of times Ah had to lift Mammy off and on the commode or even less would they appreciate a detailed account of her bowel movements.*

Set in Her Ways

Unaware that she was still smiling, Mima was surprised on entering the factory gates to hear Ethne Murphy her best pal call over: "Ah see ye're lookin a wee bit cheerier the day Mima. Is yer Mammy on the mend?"

Quickening her steps, Mima joined her friend at the same time. "Thanks for asking, Ethne, but Ah think ye ken as weel as Ah dae masell, there will never be any betterness for ma poor auld Mammy".

Her friend nodded. "Aye true enough. Ah suppose ye mean since she went aff her heid the day ye were born in the Polis Station, and her man died the very same day in some kinda accident. That right? All that was mair than enough for tae make anybody even the maist sanest person in the land, tae make them lose the place and dance awa wi the fairies.

Mima nodded. "Aye, Ethne. But like Ah say it's aye that guid of ye tae ask aboot her."

Ethne cocked her head on one side. "It's ma ain Mother, actually, if ye must know. She's aye that desperate speirin for news. The pair o them, they was big pals years ago, on the flower arranging rota and the altar-cloth washing team – that was afore yer Mammy gave up on goin tae Mass, of course."

Mima gave a rueful smile. "Ah think the sudden tragic death of ma Father changed everything for her. No tae mention that although the boys were lucky enough to escape wi their lives, once they'd recovered sufficiently from their injuries – what did they dae? Only leave her in the lurch when they scooted aff tae the Canadian Prairies and the free farmland on offer there. What wi one thing and another it wisnae just the Church she gave up on latterly."

Ethne sighed. "Weel as ma ain Mither often says – there but for the Grace of God ..."

Mima wheeled round. "Ah think ma Mammy must've felt that the Grace of God was in mighty short supply when all that doom and gloom happened tae her. And forbye, don't forget, she had tae work her fingers tae the bone for tae keep me fed, clothed and wi some kinda roof ower ma heid when Ah was a wean."

There was no answer to this, but the silence was broken when Teenie Gowan shouted over: "Hurry up, ye two, afore the Gaffer docks yer wages for being late. It's no a bloody charity they're runnin here."

This was sufficient warning to make Mima and her pal hike up their skirts and head at high speed for the doorway and the start of another day's darg.

Plenty mair work when Ah get hame, but at least here Ah get paid for it, was Mima's last thought as she rolled up her sleeves in readiness for whatever work awaited her.

There were days when Mima found it hard to believe that already she'd been working in the biscuit factory for three years. In that time most of the girls who'd started with her at the packing-station had become involved with the man of their dreams; had a quick, inexpensive and no frills courtship in any convenient back-close and then, dressed in virginal white, just made it to God's holy altar in the nick of time to keep up the hoped-for pretence of a premature baby.

It had been Mima's experience in discussing the tangled skeins of such romantic alliances that many of her friends, hell-bent on a fast track to the altar, also had another and a hidden agenda. The fact was it was common knowledge that in capturing a man, the tedium of slaving away in any factory or mill would be gone and a girl could then be her own mistress in a wee single-end.

While she worked at the bench, Mima thought: *Hmph! Some fat chance that!*

Next thing and, almost before the ink was dry on the marriage certificate, the dewy-eyed bride found herself lumbered with a drunken, lay-about husband, a hoose full o' weans a pailful of dirty nappies, a pulley creakin wi loads of drippin semmits, knickers and liberty bodices. Even worse with little or no money coming in, eventually she could not get anything as good as a factory job but instead would count herself lucky tae be oot washin stairs in wally-closes or even takin other folks washing to the steamie in order to earn a sixpence or two.

Oh no, thought Mima. *That's not the life for me, thanks all the same. Ah've enough on my hands workin here packin biscuits tae earn a shilling, then daein ma unpaid job at hame looking after ma Mammy.*

Later that same day as Mima joined a group of girls leaving the factory, Oona Brogan smirking said: "Ah see yon Frankie Weir – going hot and heavy wi some other lassie noo. Last Ah heard and saw he was makin sheep's eyes at ye, Mima."

Mima waved a dismissive hand. "Oh him! Just like all the rest – after the one thing! And when Ah wouldnae let him drag me doon the nearest back-close dunnie – the daft eejit took it as an insult tae his virile Scottish manhood – whatever the hell that was supposed tae be."

A shout of derisory laughter greeted this comment, especially when Oona almost choking with laughter said: "Virile Scottish manhood! God Almighty – Ah've heard it cried many a thing but never that."

Ribald laughter engulfed the group of girls and the final word was left to the factory's one and only elderly spinster then passing by who stuck her head into the magic circle to say with a poker face and a touch of asperity: "One thing for sure, Mima if ye had gone doon the back-court ye'd soon have found out whit the brave Frankie meant. And mibbe then ye could have spelt out the mystery of life for me. For Ah've aye wondered!"

As Tibbie turned away amid gales of laughter, she suddenly swiveled back round to deliver her parting shot: "Oh Aye! It's mibbe a mystery tae me, but frae the look o some of youse lot, Ah'd say that virile Scottish manhood, by whatever name, has already scored many a bull's eye".

With that, and head held high, Tibbie Speirs, Spinster of the Parish, marched off.

As Oona and Mima wiped away their tears of laughter, Mima said: "Looking at Tibbie – Ah suppose that could be me in a few years time – after all she looks after her demented auld Mother same as Ah dae."

Oona stared. "For heaven's sake, Mima, ye'll depress us all wi talk like that. If getting a man is the only possible escape frae this facory, then Ah'm tellin ye noo – any lad wi the dirty business on his mind can lead me tae the nearest back-close and the sooner the quicker."

Mima grinned. "Well, since ye've made up yer mind, when the big day comes at least let me be yer bridesmaid – for it's the nearest Ah'll ever get tae the altar."

Oona squeezed her arm. "Sorry, hen, but ma big sister she hasnae got a man either so she'll need tae be my bridesmaid. Would ye settle for being a flower-girl?"

Mima laughed. "Ah suppose that'll have tae dae. Anyway, by that time, if my plans work oot, Ah'm hopin tae hae left the factory and be workin at a mair fancier job. Aye, a smart lookin uniform and all. There, what dae ye think o'that – how's that for a bit of news, eh?"

Oona shook her head. "Away ye go! Never heard anything so daft. They're no takin on any mair clippies on the tramcars, noo that there's enough men back frae the war. Mind that's a pity for ye. Ye've got a sharp enough tongue in yer heid for tae yell oot, guid as any man: 'Come oan get aff the caur'."

Mima threw back her head and laughed. "Aye right. But Ah didnae mention nothing about clippies, noo did Ah?"

Oona frowned. "Weel, whit was all that about a smart uniform? As far as Ah ken, they don't let women drive the Patrick and Govan ferries neither."

As they parted company at the corner of the street, Mima called back: "Think about it! Ah'll gie ye a hint ... nice overalls, a snazzy wee cap, cake boxes tied in string, cream sponges, pineapple tarts, Eiffel towers, Empire biscuits, chocolate éclairs, shops all over Glasgow ... and the name of the shops – the initials are See Bee, *C ... B*. Get it? But nae prize for guessing the right answer. Anyway, ta-ta the noo, Ah'll need tae hurry up hame. Ma Mammy will be thinking Ah've ran away wi a sojer."

TWO

1923

Once settled in her new job at the nearest City Bakeries, seventeen-year-old Mima was finding that she loved every minute of the work. In no time at all not only was she a favourite with the regular customers, but she herself had her own specials. She delighted in memorizing the names and the particular wants, likes and dislikes of each and every one. For instance, there was Mrs Cream Sponge, Mrs Pineapple Tart and Mrs My Man Cannae Stand Chocolate Cup Cakes.

Despite the wide range of cakes, scones and pancakes available, seldom, if ever, did her customers change their regular orders. One day when the shop was rather quieter than usual, Mima discussed this aspect of the job with Miss Young, the Manageress.

The moment Mima posed the question, Miss Young gave a rather superior smile.

"Mima my dear girl, you seem to forget that I have worked my way up from the shop front counter in this business. Usually people come in to buy on a certain day of the week for a specific purpose, to accommodate some family occasion or other ... that's perhaps the day that the grandparents call on their weekly visit to see the grandchildren. Then perhaps somebody else always has their best friends round for a game of cards on a Saturday evening, hence the pineapple tarts ... and so on. I'm sure you get the picture?"

Mima nodded. Miss Young went on: "You know, the more I think about it, I do believe that in years to come people will still recall with fondness what was their favorite *C.B.* cake. We might even be establishing a family tradition of sorts with the work we do here and, of course, in all our branches throughout the City. Glasgow people as we know are famous for their sweet tooth, isn't that so?"

Again Mima nodded her agreement and Miss Young said: "I'm glad to see that you are taking such an interest in your work here, Mima. Keep on as you are currently doing: always polite and courteous to your customers, interested in their comings and goings and with always a smiling face to greet them as they come in through the door. Go on keeping up the good work making them feel welcome and that they really matter to you – carry on like that and one fine day, a few years from now, of course, but one fine day you yourself could become a branch manageress just like me. Now then, isn't that an ambition to aim for?"

At these words which Mima realized were meant to be encouraging, nevertheless Mima could feel an inner doubt: *Always a smiling face – a bit of a tall order that, for Ah don't know that Ah would always manage that, especially on the all-too-many days when Ah've had a particularly bad morning with attending to Mammy before Ah even get out of the house.*

This realization was swiftly followed by another equally gloomy thought: *And all that effort, that forced smiling, that be-nice-to-the-customer-who-is-always right charade. All that effort and play-acting for what? At the end of the day having slaved my way to the top of the career ladder, all for the rather doubtful privilege of being in charge of a bunch of silly wee girls ... every one of them just biding their time serving in the shop while waiting their first chance of capturing a husband.*

She became aware that Miss Young was again speaking to her.

"Oh! Sorry, Miss Young – what was that you just said?"

The manageress gave her a studied look, as if already regretting the rose-coloured future she had so recently painted for Mima. But rather than leave it there, in her wisdom, Miss Young held out a detaining hand. "Just one thing, Mima and a very important point – do please always remember that the vast majority of your customers have to scrimp and save every halfpenny they can in order to afford the luxury – the undoubted luxury – of our C.B. lovely cakes. So to that end, we owe it to our loyal clients to give them the very best service we can provide ..."

The manageress took a deep breath and Mima already feeling that she'd heard more than enough on the subject for one day, very daringly and quite uncharacteristically butted in to say: "Yes, thank you, Ah do understand all that, Miss Young."

The older woman looked thoughtful as she held a forefinger to her bottom lip. Finally she said: "Yes, well, as to that ... understanding is one thing. But as to the practical application. I do believe you could do with a bit more practice at tying the boxes rather more neatly. Always release the string carefully from the dispenser, then concentrate on executing a really neat bow ... nothing slipshod, you understand. After all, do not let us forget that is the way our customers carry their cake boxes by slipping the loop over a finger or two."

It was in that moment that Mima finally knew with the greatest certainty – if her future held nothing more exciting or uplifting than tying a perfect bow with a length of string – was it really all that worth striving for?

Come to think of it – before ma looks fade and Ah'm past it – why not follow the back-close route, same as all ma pals? Ah can't think why Ah've never thought of it before – but if Ah do manage to nab myself a husband – at least then Ah'll have another pair of hands to help me with Mammy. And as an added bonus, he'll be the one working and hopefully, if not too much of a drinker, he'll be bringing home a pay packet every Friday night. Now, then my girl – there's an idea!

Set in Her Ways

A voice broke into her thoughts: "Mima! That's the second time I've had to alert you today to what I am saying. I'm sorry to admit this, but your mind just does not seem to be sufficiently on your work today."

Mima turned to face her boss. "Sorry, Miss Young, it was ... you see ... my Mother she had a really bad night ... Ah was up nearly every hour with her, into the wee small hours."

Miss Young pursed her lips, all trace of the caring tutor of young minds gone. With a face like vinegar, she said, "We all have home responsibilities. I myself housekeep for my aged Father – he has a bad back you know." She allowed this bit of information to sink in, then with a brisk rubbing together of the palms of her hands, she said: "Enough of our domestic trials! Anyway, the shop has gone quieter, so not a moment to lose; quick now, let's get you practicing on tying those string-bows."

THREE

The last day of the year was slowly edging towards the hour of six o'clock when, *Glory halleluiah*, thought Mima, *the shop would close and Ah'll be free of serving – at least here in the shop.*

But she knew that once home, as usual, she would have her hands full in attending to the many needs, assorted ailments – imagined or otherwise – of her Mammy. A long sigh escaped her lips, not un-noticed by Miss Young who unusually for her did not issue an immediate reprimand.

Instead she turned to her weary assistant with the words: "Yes, Mima it has been a long and tiring day for all of us. But keep up your spirits we're nearly done now."

Lizzie, the young trainee straightened up her uniform cap. "Thank God for that. Honestly, if one more drunk man, reels in here reekin of booze and thinking he's God gift to women, flirts wi me and then in a wheedling voice asks for a Scotch pie or a flies cemetery, then Ah'll scream. Ah'm fussy Ah am and wouldnae touch one o those drunkards wi' a bargepole. And if they try any funny business, Ah'll soon tell them their bloody fortune, so Ah will."

Set in Her Ways

Miss Young frowned, instantly at her most disapproving. "I do trust that you will be rather more discreet than that, Lizzie. Of course, we all realize to our cost, that this is not our usual type of clientele – but at Hogmanay with excessive drink already taken, well, let's face it and call a spade a spade – the whole of Glasgow seems to go mad."

Lizzie by now rather shame faced replied: "Anyway, ye'd think that if the yards has closed early, they'd be wantin tae get home."

Mima and Miss Young exchanged glances and it was left to Mima to explain: "Thing is, they've already probably spent the best part of their wages in the pub, it's too early yet for the chipshops to open, and by now, they're starving o hunger. Even worse, big brave men or not, but they're scared to go home with an empty pay-poke. Anyway, their wives will be too busy frantically cleanin every inch of the house to stop off just to make a meal for the lord and master. They've just about enough money left for a pie or a cake – flies cemetery, the only name they know – so, what do they do?"

A chorus of voices from the other shop assistants: "Head for the nearest City Bakeries. They've aye heard their good wives talking about it, so that's why they end up here."

Miss Young, pleased to have her assembled staff awaiting her comment unbent sufficiently to laugh. "Yes, yes, it's true – we see this pantomime played out every single Hogmanay. Come to think of it with you being new to the job, Lizzie, perhaps I should have warned you."

Mima gave a reassuring smile to Lizzie. "Never mind, Lizzie – at least come next Hogmanay, you'll know the ropes and be ready for our annual invasion of hungry Horaces."

Far from being reassured on this point, Lizzie gave her tip-tilted cap an extra tug atop her mass of curls. "Hmph. Ye think Ah'll still be behind this counter next year? Not on yer Nellie!"

Then first having ascertained that Miss Young had now gone into the back-shop, Lizzie beckoned Mima closer and speaking behind a cupped hand, she said: "Don't for God's sake let on to her highness in there – she'd faint if she knew – but Ah'm only here in this dump until Ah can capture a man for masel. Then, for me, Ah'm the wee girl that'll be sayin: 'Goodye and good riddance, City Bakeries and hello then, china, tae wedded bliss.'"

As Mima did her level best to show the right amount of appropriate surprise at this earth-shaking confession, she knew that when the glorious day came of Lizzie's departure, the news wouldn't come as a bolt from the blue to the world-weary manageress. Yes, not only had she seen the process an endless number of times, over the years of training up young makee-learn shop assistants, by now in her own lonely and unlooked for Spinster of the Parish state – she knew without another word being said the chapter and verse of the entire so-called romantic procedure. For her all it meant – she'd need to start training up another young assistant.

FOUR

With still ten minutes to go before closing time, had Mima allowed young Lizzie to attend to the woman and girning child who arrived, breathless and clearly upset, at the counter, then all would have been well. Instead, on seeing that the woman was one of her regulars and not wishing to leave her to the rather haphazard ministrations of the couldnae-care-less Lizzie, Mima at once stepped forward in the line of duty to greet Mrs Lang. Pinning a smile to her face and displaying an enthusiasm which she was very far from feeling, Mima said: "Good evening to ye Mrs Lang. My, but ye and wee Jenny – the pair of ye, late on the road tonight surely?"

The rather flustered woman nodded. "Uch! And Ah'm the one that knows it ... in fact, Ah swithered whether or not tae come in just before ye close, ye lassies will all be in a hurry tae get home, seeing it's Hogmanay."

Mima could feel herself blush with embarrassment and rushed to say: "Oh! Dear me, Mistress Lang, Ah wasn't meaning my remark to be in any way a criticism – Ah'd hate ye to think that. And more especially with ye being a regular, indeed a valued, customer."

Set in Her Ways

As if surveying Mima through a fog the woman shook her head, then through narrowed eyes she peered more closely. "Whit's that ye were sayin? Uch! Tae tell ye the truth, hen, Ah've just had such a job getting round from Elder Street, Ah was beginning for tae think Ah wouldnae make it the nicht, never mind this year."

Mima assumed what she hoped was a vaguely interested look, by now aware that a tale of some kind was about to be related. Mrs Lang took a deep breath preparatory to speaking but even then turned and gave a hefty smack at her daughter's behind.

"Jenny! Will ye stop that snivelin, therr's naebody wants tae hear ye bawlin yer face aff."

Rather than having the desired effect of quietening the child, the opposite came out in a loud scream.

Hoping to calm things down, get the woman served with her cake order and then shut the shop, Mima said: "Ah don't believe Ah've ever seen wee Jenny this upset before – what happened, did she fall and graze her knee?"

Mrs Lang shook her head. "She's greetin because Ah smacked her bum for makin fun o poor wee, bandy-leggit Leerie."

Mima gave a knowing smile. "But Mrs Lang – all the bairns sing yon ditty about Leerie, Leerie, light the lamps, wi yer lang pole and crooked shanks."

The customer tightened her lips. "Aye, true enough and Ah've often heard it shouted in the streets after him. But see that wee lamplighter, he's a giant among men. For what he's did the night, he's a hero; a hero, Ah say."

Mima still feeling slightly less than interested gave a vaguely encouraging tilt of her head and Mrs Lang went on: "Ye'll never believe what happened – it was a drunken fight outside yon pub, wi two drunk men on the pavement knocking the hell oota each other – Ah tell ye – one man's face already lookin like a pun o mince. Anyway, we couldnae get past and Jenny she's scared o drunk men – her Da and her Grandpaw signed the Pledge and go every week tae the Band of Hope, tae see all yon lantern slides about the evils o the Demon Drink. Anyway, we're trapped in a corner of the pavement; Jenny's screamin her heid off – nae escape!"

Mima by now desperate to put an end to this catalogue of disaster, make a quick sale and head for a cup of tea, said: "Ah suppose Leerie shouted at them to get out of the way and let ye past."

Mrs Lang's eyes widened. "Ah can see it yet! Ye'll never guess, brave wee man that he is ... what does he dae? He jist wachles over bandy-leggit or no, calm as ninepence, gets near the two eejits still battlin it out on the pavement and then starts poking his lamplighter's pole intae both the pair of them. He might look a wee shilpit man – no' his fault he got rickets as a wean – but in that hour of oor need, Leerie the lamplighter was brave as Wallace the Bruce himsel."

The tale now finally told, and having shown the appropriate expression of wonder on her face, Mima then rubbed her hands together. "Now then, Mrs Lang, Ah'm glad all ended safely for ye and like ye say, that wee man deserves a medal. Anyway, to turn to other matters – if it's yer usual flies cemeteries ye're after, sorry, but Ah think we've only one of them left."

Mrs Lang opened her eyes wide with alarm. "Oh! help ma boab! Don't tell me that. See my man – he'll murder me, especially on Hogmanay, if he cannae get his favourite sweet-bites. Just the one cake wilnaedae it for him, that'll hardly touch the sides o his stomach. He fair loves his sweet bites."

A barely suppressed giggle and a muttered comment which sounded suspiciously like something to do with love-bites from Lizzie who was clearly more streetwise than she was letting on, alerted both Mima and her regular customer. As the unfortunate comments faded away, at once all enraged housewife and keeper of her daughter's moral wellbeing, Mrs Lang turned and said: "Excuse me, Miss whatever yer name is – have Ah just said something funny?"

In that moment, sensing that things could very soon get ugly and with no saviour of a bandy wee lamplighter immediately on hand to work his pole-wielding magic, Mima entered the fray. "Uch, just ignore her, Mrs Lang, she's supposed to be meeting her new lumber the night – a big handsome, kilted Highlander by all accounts – and it's gone to her head – she's been giggling away and talking rubbish like that all afternoon. Lizzie, into the back shop with ye now, and finish cleaning up." As Lizzie beat a hasty retreat, Mima said: "She's just a daft young lassie, cannae wait to get married and get out of working in this City Bakeries hell-hole. They're all the same and who could blame them – who in their right mind would want to work here?"

Looking at the departing back of Lizzie, Mrs Lang then turned back to face Mima and said: "That lassie was being cheeky tae me, ye were a wee bit too quick in letting her off the hook. Ah'd soon have given that pert young miss a piece of my mind."

With no quick answer to this, Mima kept a discreet silence and Mrs Lang went on: "But come to think of it – Ah've got a bone tae pick with ye as weel."

Mima frowned. "Oh! really? Ah'm sorry to hear that, Mrs Lang, Ah really cannot see that Ah could have offended ye in any way."

"Offended me? Oh, ye've done worser than that my fine lady, ye've just spoiled the life ambition of my wee Jenny here."

Mima frowned, completely at a loss as to what on earth the red-faced woman was going on about. "Ah'm sorry – Ah really do not have a single clue as to what –"

Mrs Lang, by now all motherly concern for her still-snivelling, runny-nosed wean, bent down, smoothed her daughter's hair then straightened up and said: "Ah demand for tae see the Manageress of this establishment."

As luck, or an evil-minded fate, would have it, just at that moment, Miss Young appeared again in the front shop. "Something I can help you with, Madam?"

Mrs Lang pointed a trembling forefinger at Mima and said: "Aye, since ye ask, ye can give yer assistant here a bit of a ticking-off. She's just called this fine shop nothin other than a hell-hole of a place to work in."

Miss Young drew herself to her full height. "I'm sure there must be some misunderstanding, Madam. We are all tired, it's been a long day and by rights, instead of letting you in at the last minute, we should have shut up shop twenty minutes ago. A misunderstanding, right?"

Mrs Lang's brow beetled.

"Misunderstanding, be damned. Thing is ma wee Jenny she's bright, a clever wee lass roon at Greenfield School, the teacher thinks highly of her – and Jenny had set her heart on one day being old enough tae get a job in here. And wear that swanky wee uniform and cap like the rest o' youse. And noo, bein telt this is a hell-hole. Just look at the wee darling, her ambitions shattered, fair breakin her innocent wee heart, so she is."

As Miss Young and Mima both looked at the pitiful sight of the snotty-nosed, green-slime dripping wean, Mima felt moved to say: "City Bakeries being a hell-hole or not has nothing, Ah repeat nothing whatsoever to do with wee Jenny's distress. She's been crying like a banshee since she came into the shop, Mrs Lang and more especially after ye gave her an almighty whack to her bahookie."

Mrs Lang sucked in her breath. "Haud on a meenit, Mima. Are ye now saying that Ah've laid a hand on my bairn? Are ye sayin Ah'm a bad Mother?"

Miss Young, now also looking rather flushed turned to face Mima and said: "I just cannot imagine what vile untruths have been spouted. But enough! Mima – tie off Mrs Lang's box of cakes and let us have done with this. Then the matter ends here – all's well that ends well, as my dear Granny used to say."

Anything for a quiet life, thought Mima.

Then about to tie the final elaborate bow in the string securing the cake-box, Mima stopped short "Miss Young – put it this way – Ah don't give tuppence for what yer Granny used to say. And as to the vile untruths ye were on about – ye can believe any damned thing ye like. Right now, Ah'm too tired, too fed-up and altogether too bone-weary to start any investigation – official or otherwise – into who said what, when they said it or even why. But here's something Ah will say – as of now, this very minute, Ah am out of here and ye can take yer sainted job, yer petty rules and regulations and stuff them up yeur jacksy, for all Ah care." As Mima finished speaking, she wrenched off her City Bakeries emblazoned uniform cap off her head, then holding it out to the irate customer, she yelled: "And if as ye say – and God help her if it's the case – if this is wee Jenny's heart's desire – then here, she's welcome to my cap of office. Ah just hope it'll bring her more joy and fulfilment than it ever did me."

Miss Young put out a restraining hand, but Mima would have none of it. "My mind is made up, Ah just wish Ah'd spoke up sooner. Anyway – a Happy New Year to youse all when it comes. See me? Ah'm away home to put on my nurse's badge of office and attend to my poor old Mother. Away in the fairies she might be, but daft or not, somehow she managed to bring me up to look after her in her old age. And at least she appreciates my efforts. Good bye."

FIVE

1925

Now out of a job and without so much as a single reference of any kind to her name, Mima soon learned the untimely haste of her ways.

If only Ah'd bit my lip and said nothing, instead of being so smart and sounding off to all and sundry like that. But to do myself justice, Ah suppose what with one thing and another Ah was just at the end of my tether when Mrs Lang started bemoaning the loss of wee Jenny's rose-coloured City Bakeries future!

And the more Mima thought about it, the more she realized just how very much she now missed the comfortable, albeit hardworking regime she'd had at the City Bakeries. Then too, of course, having so often basked in the warm approval and encouragement of Miss Young, the current lack of appreciation from any single living soul now made her life seem barren, arid and totally lacking in purpose of any meaningful kind. About to dwell even further on such dark, gloomy thoughts, Mima came out of her reverie to the sound of her Mother yelling: "Mima! Mima! Ah'm Ah tae be left sittin here abandoned, on ma throne all day? And wi no even ma bum wiped!"

Set in Her Ways

Mima turned her head and as if seeing her Mother for the first time, she studied the twisted, angry, petulant face now confronting her. With a sigh born of frustration, Mima started on the first of their daily rituals as with a wedge of cut-newspaper squares clutched in her hand, she approached her Mother. Minutes later, the essential cleaning operation over to her Mother's satisfaction, Mima would fain have sat down by the fireside for a few minutes respite. But as she already knew, that was the pipe-dream. The stark reality was that any second now, like a demanding toddler, her Mother would start banging a spoon on the table, as an accompaniment to her sorrows chanting: "Porridge, porridge, Ah'm wantin porridge."

Mima knowing well the routine was aware that if she was not quick enough to attend to this particular dietary need, then next would come the inevitable and equally soul-destroying chant of, "A poor auld bodie could die o hunger in this hoose. Fair starving, so Ah am. Ma stomach thinks ma throat's cut, so it does."

Almost like a chunk of learned-by-heart rhetoric of ancient poetry or even the Psalms of David, this would be repeated word for word, perfect until the blessed moment of delivery when at last, the bowl of porridge placed on the table before her Mother, the latter would stop speaking and shouting and instead start the equally noisy activity of slurpin up her favourite comestible.

As Mima continued to gaze on this breakfast scene, she thought: *Ah'll have to get another job. And damned quick about it. And not just for the money — essential though that surely is — but at least when Ah'm working then Ah do have a valid excuse to leave Mother alone each day. And let's face it, but if Ah don't manage to escape from this cesspit for at least a part of everyday out of sound, sight and smell of her and her many needs, then Ah'll go stark, starin mad. The City Bakeries a hell-hole? Never in a million years! Compared to this, the City Bakeries was a paradise on earth.*

As the days, weeks and months of Mima's jobless state went by and the precious store of farthings, halfpennies and silver threepenny bits diminished, Mima felt she was becoming more and more desperate to find employment, gainful employment of any kind. But with so few jobs, gainful or otherwise, available and so many unemployed people every bit as frantic as Mima to earn an honest crust, each attempt, no matter how robustly tackled seemed to be doomed to failure right from the word go.

It was after yet another week of fruitless, soul-destroying job searching that it finally happened. That particular Saturday morning with icicles even on the inside of their one and only window, Mima had mentally decided, *That's enough for this week. It must be freezing cold out there, so here's what Ah'm gonnae do. Ah'm gonnae treat myself to a day by the fireside. Then after a week-end of cooterin myself up,*

Set in Her Ways

Ah'll feel strong enough that come Monday morning, Ah'll set out yet again, with head and hopes held high to go on the job hunt.

It seemed that no sooner had Mima decide on her day or two of spoiling, than her Mother almost as if by some weird means catching the unspoken message that for once, she would have Mima's undivided attention – then became at her most childlike, demanding and difficult. If it wasn't one thing she wanted, it was another. Then having got her heart's desire of a wee bit of bread toasted at the fire she then threw the bobby-dazzler of all tantrums because with not a scrape of syrup on treacle left in the house, she screamed in frustration: "Uch! How am Ah supposed for tae get ma auld gnashers through a bit, dry as a desert, burnt black toast."

As her Mother sat with her arm raised, as if poised to chuck the offending bread at her daughter, Mima got into the act first. She lunged forward, grabbed hold of the offending burnt, and loudly-rejected, offering and then she stopped short.

To her utter horror, she realized in that moment that in a white blaze of anger, she had been within an ace of ramming the toast – ramming it hard with all the power at her disposal – right down into her Mother's still-open mouth. As she suddenly realized the enormity, the venomous intent of what she had so recently mentally proposed to do, she paused, already aghast and trembling at the wild anger she had unleashed. She looked at her Mother's now stricken face, stared unseeingly at the toast she still held in her hand, and then with the last vestige of her strength, she tossed the bread into the fire.

Then, reason having finally prevailed, she turned to her Mother and said: "A word of warning for yer own good. Don't ye dare say a single word. Not one more word do Ah want to hear from ye today."

Her Mother frowned. "But ..."

Mima again approached until she was eyeball-to-eyeball with her Mother. Then pointing an accusatory forefinger, Mima said quietly but forcefully: "But me no butts, Mother. If ever anybody needed the patience of a Saint, it's surely me – but let's face it, even a Saint has limits of endurance and tolerance."

"But ye surely don't expect me to –"

Mima could feel the muscles of her face contorting into a frown. "What Ah expect is that ye'll content yerself, ye've had yer porridge, ye don't want yer toast. So now, just sit here quietly have a wee bit snooze and let me go off outside intae the cold to look for a job."

Once happed up with her shawl and crouched against a cruel, biting wind Mima made her way aimlessly through the city streets. As she slithered her away along the ice-caked pavements, she wondered: *Already Ah've tried every possible shop, mill and manufactory – but nobody wants or needs me, in even the meanest category of labour. God help me, where do Ah go from here?*

A voice broke into her thoughts and as Mima raised her head, she was surprised to find herself looking into the rather concerned eyes of Tibbie Speirs, the in-with-the-bricks old maid from the biscuit factory.

"Ah said and Ah'll say it again – Mima ye're getting mair and mair like yer auld Mother every time Ah see ye – and here ye are noo even talking tae yersell – and oot in the public street of all places. Whit next, whit next – that's what Ah'm askin masell."

Mima raised her eyes to heaven. "Thanks for those kind words, Tibbie – that's really cheered me up this day. And if Ah'm getting mair liker ma Mammy – nae better person – when Ah think what she went through and yet still overcame it, somehow tae bring me up decent, honest, fed and clothed – at least until Ah was old enough tae take care of her."

Tibbie grinned. "Glad tae hae been o service. Anyway, ye can get aff yer high horse noo. Fine weel Ah ken yer Maw's had a raw deal frae life and the Man upstairs – so, can we just forget it noo? But tell me this and tell me nae mair – whit in the name o the wee man were ye chunteren on about when Ah bumped intae ye? Ah'm no exactly deaf as a post yet, but even so, Ah couldnae quite make oot whit ye was sayin."

"God Almighty – Ah think Nosey Parker must be yer middle-name. Weel, if ye must know and if it'll shut yer geggie – Ah was wondering tae masell, oot loud, Ah suppose, just debating as to where on God's earth in the City o Glesga, Ah could get a job o some kind. Ah'm fair desperate for work – and that's a fact."

Tibbie nodded "Aye – ye and the rest o all the Glesga Keelies. There's no over many jobs goin abeggin these days." A silence fell between the two women, then suddenly Tibbie said: "Hold on a meenit, china – noo Ah come come tae think of it – but Ah believe mibbe Ah could help ye in yer hour of need, like."

Mima waited hopefully but at the same time fully aware as to how often those self-same hopes had been dashed in recent months.

Tibbie, her thinking face on, mentally considered whatever scheme was then racing through her head. At last, she nodded then beckoning Mima closer she whispered: "Dae ye mind yon Janetta Burns? Weel, Ah see she's fallen again – the rate she's producing bairns, her man must be at it night and day – he disnae work, ye see – but anyway, here's what Ah'm getting at. She did tell me that him wi his bad back and all and no able tae work – she has a whole lot o bits-n-pieces o jobs. But right now, what wi the worst morning sickness she's ever had – all her bad days, her squad o'weans, a no-weel man and one thing and another, she's finding it real hard tae cope wi all her wee jobs."

Mima frowned. "What dae ye mean, all her jobs – surely naebody – this day and age has mair than the one job?"

Tibbie tapped the side of her nose in a grand theatrical gesture which she clearly thought indicated that she was about to divulge a secret, a juicy bit of gossip or at the very least, an outpouring of superior knowledge of some kind unknown to lesser human beings.

The mystery was soon revealed and although Tibbie went all round the houses to explain every nuance of the circumstances, the gist of it, as Mima finally understood it was: a now heartily pregnant Janetta – "Ye mind her from yer days at the biscuit factory." – was now unable to fulfil the weekly household duties she did for a group of Jewish families, in preparation for their Sabbath, their Holy Day on which no fires could be cleaned, lit or stoked and no cooking pots could be scoured. The message which came loud and clear was that if Mima cared to hand over a wee bit siller to Janetta – "Something like the key-money ye give a factor" – then the job would be Mima's – at least until Janetta had produced her latest bairn and was again fit and well enough to resume her paid duties in the Jewish households.

The key-money – For want of a better word, thought Mima – having been duly handed over, Mima soon found that the new job and the small remuneration it brought into the household purse suited her admirably. Not only could she fit in the required hours of work around the care she had of necessity to bestow on her Mother, the new job had one other distinct advantage. It gave her the added, and above all, the perfectly legitimate excuse for a few hours of escaping from the increasingly cantankerous and hard to please old woman such as her Mother had now become.

Although Mima still worried about and felt sorry for her Mother, the fact remained that deep down and ever conscious of the debt of gratitude for her upbringing, she loved her Mother dearly. All of which Mima found difficult to cope with on the many occasions when loving her or not her Mother was at her most demanding, Mima would find herself thinking: *Honestly! There must be a thin dividing line between love and hate — there's times Ah could quite cheerfully throttle the auld besom.*

As if this wasn't bad enough, with the constant overhanging threat that any week now Janetta would be taking back her old job and with it would go the only money coming into the Reilly household, Mima knew she would have to do something, anything to keep the pair of them out of the workhouse.

Such were the thoughts surging through her brain that very morning when on her way round to Coburg Street to attend to the usual needs of her Jewish families, she was yet again hailed by Sandy, the local postman. As he chatted on boringly about the vagaries of the Scottish climate, with particular reference to Glasgow, Mima was already forming an idea in her mind.

Why not? she wondered. *It isn't as if Ah've got two heads and the way he keeps meeting me accidentally, Ah really do think he fancies me!*

It was several months later and Mima's Mother away in the fairies or not, still had moments of intense clarity and sound common sense.

Fixing Mima with a piercing glare, her Mother repeated for about the tenth time in as many minutes: "Ye say this Sandy, whatever his name is, this postie-fella, he's actually wantin for tae marry ye!" Her Mother shook her head in wonder and went on: "And ye tell me he's a widower – that right? Weel, Ah'd watch it if Ah was ye – there will be only the one thing he's after, and we all know what that is. Forbye, he's a man, he's not daft, and with an eye tae the main chance, he's probably lining ye up for tae be his nursemaid in his auld age – ye did say, he's a bit older than ye. One way and another, no much of an outlook for ye then, is it ... bed-mate, cleaner, cook, washer-woman and at the end, his ain personal nurse and handmaiden?"

She stopped for breath and Mima sighed. "Uch, Mother can ye no be happy for me? Anyway, one thing ye're forgettin – a guid-livin man with a steady pay-packet about the hoose, he'd dae us both a power of good."

Her Mother's reply was to deliver herself of a satisfying belch followed by the words: "Like Ah say, if Ah was ye ..."

Mima wiped the globules of porridge from her Mother's chin.

"Put it this way, Mother ... ye're not me and if Ah've captured masell a man in spite of all yer gloomy interference, that's my business. And for yer information, Ah can tell ye right here and now, if what's worrying ye is that we'll need tae move tae another hoose – that's not going to happen. Ma Sandy has already telt me that he'd be mair than happy tae live here, in with us and it would be a lot handier for him tae get tae his work than where he is livin noo."

Silence greeted this then her Mother smirked. "Oh! So now the poor man is ma Sandy is he? My, my!

SIX

1926

The first anniversary of their marriage had come and gone and despite or perhaps even because of all her Mother's misgivings, Mima felt she had never been happier in her whole life. She hummed to herself as she cleared away the breakfast clutter.

Mima MacRae, ye're in high spirits this morning – great what having a kindly, considerate, pay-poke handing-in man about the hoose can dae for ye. Should mibbe have tried the marriage state sooner!

Her Mother's voice called out across the room: "That ye goin on again, talking tae yersel about that man, that postie fella."

Mima turned. "He's not just any man. He's my man, my man. And he does have a name. High time ye stopped referring to him as that postie fella. He's my Sandy, Sandy MacRae and if ye don't already know it – Ah'll tell ye again …"

Her Mother sighed. "Whit noo?"

Mima stood arms akimbo. "Just so ye know – Ah bless the very hour and day he put this wedding ring on my finger."

Her Mother gave a derisory snort. "Ye've certainly changed yer tune my fine lady. Ah've heard ye, so Ah have – nothing wrong with my hearing – heard ye talking tae yer pal Janetta – in this very hoose – her cryin her man every name under the sun for knockin oot a bairn every year like clock work – and ye, runnin doon yer beloved postie fella, somethin about his drunkin fumblins and gropins on a Saturday night and still he cannae get ye in the family way."

Mima could feel the hot colour of embarrassment rush into her cheeks. "Mother! That's scandalous talk, even to mention such private matrimonial matters and Ah'll not listen tae another word. Anyway, like Ah say, Ah'm happy, happier than Ah've ever been and ye can put this in yer pipe and smoke it – Ah count masel a lucky, a very lucky woman."

No sooner had Mima voiced this opinion to her less than interested Mother, than suddenly she felt a frisson of fear – *was she somehow tempting fate by declaring so emphatically and so publicly that she was happy in the married state, especially since to date, it had, more or less, all been plain sailing on their tranquil sea of matrimony.*

Still mentally debating as to whether or not she had tempted fate Mima was brought back into the here and now when her Mother said: "If ye're happy, then ye must be easily pleased – that postie-fella, he's that tight with his money to him every farthing's a prisoner – he couldnae even buy ye a new wedding ring – used his dead wife's auld ring – cheap!"

SEVEN

1927

The year 1927 opened with winds of over 100 mph lashing Scotland and causing absolute chaos in many parts of the country. As Sandy went about as usual delivering letters in the teeth of the gale, Mima constantly worried for his safety especially as with each hour that passed more and more trees were being blown down. Even tramcars overturned in the streets and hundreds of buildings suffered structural damage resulting in slates, chimney heads and even the debris from collapsing tenements falling into the streets. As a decidedly storm-tossed Sandy arrived home from work that evening the moment he came in the door, Mima flew to his side and threw her arms around him.

"Thank God, thank God, ye're home safely, oh my lovely man, Sandy, ye're safe. Ah've worried myself sick all day, that wind's been screamin – Ah even thought our window was going tae heave in at one point. Oh, Sandy!"

As her husband disentangled himself from her embrace, he grinned in a rather embarrassed fashion, then seeking to deflate the situation by way of a joke, he said: "Haud aff on with all the kissin and cuddlin, Mima – this is only just Thursday – no Saturday night."

Mima smiled. "Oh aye—see what ye mean. But listenin tae that howlin wind all day – it fair terrified me."

Sandy held her at arm's length. "So it should scare ye. According tae what it says in The Daily Record it's no just a strong wind – it's a bloody hurricane so it is. Seems that with a wind speed of 102 m.p.h. it's the strongest gusts ever noted in Scotland and recorded at the Paisley Observatory since records began there back in 1883."

Mima gasped in amazement. "Dae ye tell me that noo, Sandy?"

He nodded, pleased to have a captive audience and went on: "Ye think that's bad – just wait 'til Ah tell ye this – Ah've even saw a tramcar, wheeched over like a wee bit o paper and noo lyin in the street. What dae ye think o'that? Ah've never saw nothing like it in all ma born days. They say there's even folk trapped underneath it."

Mima shivered. "Oh! my God – that could hae been ye, Sandy. There'll be heartbreak at somebody's door this night – Ah hope it's naebody we know. Oh, Sandy, don't tell me any more – Ah'm just that glad tae have ye hame safe and sound."

Again she lunged into his arms and stayed like that until her Mother called out: "If that's ye two lovebirds done with all that cuddlin and canoodlin – mibbe before an auld bodie like me dies o' hunger, mibbe Ah could get a drink o tea and a soda scone."

The year which had come in so dramatically with a hurricane was fast drawing to a close. As Mima bustled about the kitchen cleaning everything to within an inch of its life, in readiness for Hogmanay she was singing away right happily.

Not for the first time, this over-loud evidence of her joy in life seemed to irk her Mother who finally shouted: "For heaven's sake, Mima – can ye no just shut yer geggie for ten minutes at a time. Ye're fair giving me a headache with all that damned racket. Forbye, any minute noo, if Ah'm no careful, ye'll start dustin me." Determined not to allow her Mother to spoil her mood, Mima, with a supreme effort of will, smiled sweetly. "Now there's an idea – mibbe Ah should smarten ye up a bit before Sandy gets home. What about a wee ribbon in yer hair – that would tosh ye up for Hogmanay."

For once, her Mother cackled with laughter and made such a noise that it was a second or two before they heard someone chapping at the door. On opening the door, Mima was surprised to see Big Donald Tavish, a work companion of her husband's. Still chuckling at the image, the mental image of a ringletted, ribbon-skewered Mother in her Hogmanay finery, Mima said: "Ye're a bit early yet for the Bells, Donald. Sandy's no even back from his work yet, but we'll be right glad to see ye later."

On the point of again closing the door, she stopped when Big Donald tugging at the cloth-cap in his hand, as if holding on to a life-line, gave it an extra twist and said: "Sorry, hen, ye don't understand but that's the point – it's Sandy – he'll no be comin home the night. He's in ... they've took him tae the Royal Infirmary." Mima glared at the hapless man, who cleared his throat and pushed past her into the room. "Ah don't know how to tell ye, hen. But seems it was the simplest thing in the world – two doors on a landing tied together with a length of rope – a trick the bairns try all the time ..."

Mima nodded. "Uch that! That's nuthin – done that masell when Ah was a wean – tie the doors, ring both the doorbells and then run like hell before the housewives try tae open their doors. Nae harm in that, surely. And Sandy, he's well up tae all their tricks."

Big Donald hung his head. "True enough! And in the normal way, he's careful and would be helpful and untie the door knobs. But tonight, rushing tae get home early for his Hogmanay – well, somehow he fell over the rope and catapulted all his length doon the flight o stone steps and hurted himself."

Mima put a trembling hand to her brow. "What! He what! Oh! ma bonnie man. Ah'll need tae go tae him."

Donald put out a restraining hand. "Afore ye go, he's ..."

Mima screamed. "He's dead – is that what ye're trying tae tell me – he's dead!"

"Calm yersel, Mistress MacRae – he's still in the land o the livin but only just. And ye should know – they think he's broke his back. He'll never walk again, he's gonnae be a ..."

Mima clutched at Donald's arm. "Are ye sayin what Ah think ye're sayin – no it cannae be true, no my fine upstanding Sandy ..."

Donald nodded and gave her hand a reassuring squeeze. "Sorry, hen, sorry tae be the bearer o such bad news – but yer man, Sandy, he's gonnae be a ... cripple for the rest o his born days."

"God help Sandy and God help me. Ah'll need tae become his carer he'll have tae depend on me for everything and Ah'll have tae be the wage earner. What a bloody life! Like it or not but Ah'll be the carer for both the two of them – poor Sandy, poor Mammy, and poor me. Some Hogmanay this."

EIGHT

By the time Sandy came out of hospital and was installed back home ... a broken man whose working days were over, already Mima was beginning to show. Each time she glanced down at her bulging belly, she could not resist the thought: *Ah'd been planning to break the happy news to him that Hogmanay. Hmph. Some hopes of that. Instead Ah was the one to get news ... and nothing happy aboot it. Ah had the shock, the mind-numbing shock of hearing aboot Sandy's accident, such a simple unforeseen event and yet what a calamitous outcome. Oh God, even now Ah can hardly bear to think of it.*

Without realising, Mima must have been muttering and this dawned on her when her Mother said: "Mima, Mibbe try to keep yer voice down a bit, Ah think Sandy has dozed off in his chair."

Mima raised her head. "Aye right ye are. Thanks for that, Mammy. Ye know Ah still cannae get over it ... the way ye take such good care of ma man. Ever since his accident and noo that ye no longer can cry him that postie fella, anybody would think he's yer ain son. Changed days, eh no, Mammy?"

Set in Her Ways

Her Mother laughed. "Aye, changed days right enough. Ah think it was the shock, the suddenness of his accident, somehow it seemed tae rattle up ma brains as weel. Ah cannae right explain it."

Mima waved a dismissive hand. "Don't even try, Mammy, just leave things as they are. For ye're a changed woman, changed for the better Ah might say since that terrible night. For goodness sake look at ye, a ribbon in yer hair, sittin up nice as ninepence in yer bed and here ye are even back at the crocheting. See that shawl that ye're workin on, it's gonnae be one real lovely gift for the baby whenever he or she arrives."

Her Mother smiled and basking in the warmth of such praise, preened, gave a self-conscious pat at her piled-up, beribboned hair and said with a catch in her voice: "Call me daft if ye like, but forever more Ah'll wear a ribbon in ma hair, it reminds me of that night; for the first time ye and me suddenly we understood each other ... an accident, a terrible accident but ye see whereas ma man dies, yer Sandy is the lucky one still in the land of the livin, thank God. And somehow it's given ye and me a sort of common bond, if Ah can call it that. Dae ye get the drift of what Ah'm tryin tae tell ye?"

Mima, knowing that she was choked with emotion could not trust herself to speak. Instead she merely nodded. Then lifting a corner of the crocheted shawl, she smoothed it lovingly with her fingertips.

Yes, she thought, *times will be hard and the good Lord above knows where we'll get siller enough to feed us all, but one thing is certain sure, ma wee baby will be well-loved. And love, that's the one thing that all the money in the world cannae buy.*

NINE

SEPTEMBER 1928

Summer had come and gone almost without notice in the City's streets and now with the trees already changing colour in Glasgow Green the day and hour of Mima's labour was fast approaching.

Labour? thought Mima, *Hmph. Ah've known all aboot that these past few months, what with working every hour God sends at all ma wee jobs trying to save a wee bit of money to tide us over for when the baby comes. But the other kind of labour, pushing a baby out into the world, now, that's something else again.*

As Mima stood stock still with duster clutched in one hand and the other hand on her enormous belly she suddenly heard a voice at her elbow: "Ah said and Ah'll say it again, for God's sake don't let her ladyship see ye standin aboot idle. She's payin us good money tae clean up her hoose before her posh son arrives from Edinburgh."

Mima turned to face her friend and work-companion.

"Seems tae me, ye're more of a slave-driver than the lady of the hoose hersel. And listen Janetta, here's a wee bit of advice frae me to ye ... better no let her catch ye referrin to her guid self as her ladyship. No' but what with all her airs and graces, Ah sometimes think we should be curtseying tae her."

The two friends giggled, especially when Janetta said: "See ye, damn all curtseying ye'd manage wi that bloody great cargo ye're totin aroun in front of ye."

As their laughter died away, Janetta frowned slightly. "Anyway, Mima, what was it ye were ponderin when ye stopped workin and was just gazing intae the middle distance like some glaikit numptie."

Mima pursed her lips, uncertain as to how much of her private thoughts and worries she could or should unload on to her friend. A moment's silence, then, after an encouraging nod from Janetta, Mima having taken a deep breath, said: "It's like this, if ye must know, Ah'm scared, cannae stop thinking aboot all the horrible auld wives tales aboot childbirth."

Janetta put her hands on hips. "Uch, nae need tae keep sich worries tae yersell, hen. After all, wi the squad o kids Ah've got … if anybody's an expert on bloody childbirth, it has tae be me. Ah've had one damned labour every year since the Priest joined us thegither until death do us part."

Mima put out a hand. "Don't tell me ye've fallen again."

Janetta gave a knowing smirk. "Never again, Mima, never again. Efter that last time, Ah telt him, tie a knot in it. Go and see Durty Annie

54

when ye feel the need, dae whit ye like, but just don't come within within firin distance o me."

Mima could feel herself blush at such frank revelations about her friend's marriage and matrimonial arrangements. In an effort to divert the conversational route, Mina said: "So what ye're really tellin.me is this ... childbearin is such agony, that ye want no further part in it?"

Janetta shook her head impatiently. "Honestly, Mima, ye're a reasonably intelligent woman, ye could have been a City Bakeries manageress, for heavens sake, but ye can fair twist round a person's words."

Mima cocked her head on one side. "All right, let's hear ye untwist them and quick aboot it before the baith o us gets the sack."

Janetta took a step closer until they were eyeball to eyeball. "Childbearin is certainly nae piece of cake. It can be gey painful, that's true enough, but as tae all the tales aboot week-long labours, a lot of bloody nonsense that."

Mima opened her mouth to speak but Janetta rushed in with: "Mair to the point ... have ye given any thought as tae the geography of the big event ... efter all ye cannae be lyin screamin yer heid aff wi yer legs up in the air in yer single-end wi yer auld Mother and yer crippled man havin ringside seats."

Mima nodded. "Ah see what ye mean."

It was a few days later when the two women walking home from their cleaning jobs in wally-close-land again debated the question of where precisely the actual birth should or could be taking place. And above all, if it was to be in Mima's own home, what was to happen to the other two incumbents? As Mima stuttered confused ideas, Janetta broke in: "Forget all those cockeyed ideas, here's what ye'll dae. The minute yer waters break —"

"What? What in the name of God are ye talkin aboot, how did burst pipes suddenly come intae it? Ah don't think Ah could cope with a plumber just then."

Janetta roared with laughter. "Mima, dae ye ken nuthin aboot the laws of nature? It fair beats me how ye ever got duffed up in the first place. The minute yer labour starts, ye'll dae one almighty big streamie guid as any cart horse oot in the streets, nae holdin it back, that's yer waters breakin – yer bairn announcin it's on its way into this world."

Mima nodded and Janetta continued: "Right, the minute ye've streamied yersell, get yersell, drookit drawers an all across the landin tae me. Ah'll send ma weans over tae keep yer Maw and yer man company, they could mibbe aw play a wee game of 'Ah Spy' or sumthin tae keep themsels busy until ye've finished yer ain important business."

Mima grinned. "Ah can just see ma Mother and Sandy enjoyin an afternoon or an evening like that."

Janetta laughed. "Put it this way, hen, ye'll no exactly be havin a time of pure enjoyment yersell, so all hands tae the pump. And before ye ask, ma ain man, he'll dae what Ah tell him tae dae. If there's one place in the Gorbals he knows, apart from the pub, it's the street the midwife lives in. He can go and get a haud o her. Might as well make hissell useful."

TEN

If Janetta had been an army general commanding her troops, she could not have made a better job of the operation. The fact of her being what was locally referred to as a strong madam helped in that the minute she said, jump, then from decrepit old men to snotty nosed weans, everyone leapt to instant attention. And since she had decreed that a game of 'Ah Spy' was to be the order of the day, then it would have taken a brave heart to suggest that they might prefer the rather more exciting pastime of 'Hangman' or even the more energetic 'Cats' Cradle'.

Right from the first tinkle of Mima's breaking waters, everything went like clockwork. The moment Mima squelched her way across the landing of the close, Janetta, good as any hospital dragon of a Matron, coped with the early stages; ordered her man to go and collect the self-styled midwife; was on hand to mop with a vinegar-soaked hanky Mima'a perspiring brow and generally made herself useful. Almost as if scared to upset all of her friend's fine planning, Mima's labour, far from being of the feared week-long variety of local legend, instead was remarkably quick and comparatively easy. One long final push, one cry which reverbrated throughout the tenement and suddenly the child was born. As Mima held her son in her arms she could feel the tears of such exquisite joy coursing down her face that the raw emotion of the moment threatened to overpower her. She swallowed hard a couple of times, then after thanking midwife Ruby and master-planner Janetta, Mima said: "We decided on names ages ago, Andrew for a boy and Andrina should it have been a girl. But somehow Sandy was sure he'd be having a son."

Ruby smiled. "And a fine bouncing baby boy he is, yer son Andrew."

While Ruby and Mima had been chatting and admiring the baby, Janetta had briefly left the room. When she came back she was accompanied by her eldest daughter, who at once gazed down in wonder at her newly-born neighbour. Janetta, placing a hand on Bella's shoulder said: "Bella here was wondering, could she have the honour o carryin in wee Andrew to meet his Daddy and his Granny? They're both fair desperate to see him."

As Mima watched her friend and young Bella bear the precious bundle off in triumph, she gave a deep sigh of contentment: "Yes, Life is good, Ah have a healthy son with the requisite number of fingers and toes. Ah have a son, who could ask for more?"

ELEVEN

Never in the annals of Thistle Street had there ever been a better, bonnier or more contented baby than wee Andrew MacRae. From the moment he opened his baby blue eyes in the morning in his chest of drawers makeshift cot, until he closed them again in slumber at day's end, his presence was pure delight.

And quite apart from his doting Granny, Daddy and Mammy, always nearby would be a willing army of equally-captivated wee girls eager to take him out for a walk in the decidedly battered looking pram, a haud-me-doon conveyance which had previously served the needs of many a Gorbals family. For those not lucky enough to be entrusted with this sacred duty of pram pushing, but ever willing to assist in some way, they were happy to run errands for Mima. Then in the fullness of time, when allowed to accompany the then official pram-pusher, such admirers were proud to have one proprietary hand on the handle of Andrew's baby-carriage as they walked in stately procession along the city streets.

Aye, thought Mima, *It's all a grand help to me, otherwise with all ma wee bits of cleanin jobs and Andrew's home-locked Daddy and Granny, it would be many a long day before such an outing, a fresh air outing would be possible.*

At this thought Mima couldn't help a smile rising to her lips. *Not that there's all that much actual fresh air in the streets around Gorbals Cross, but at least it does get him out of the house for a wee while.*

As Mima settled her son in his pram complete with a lovely new crocheted blanket his Granny had made for him, she turned to Lena and her eager young assistant. "Now remember girls, take extra care when crossing the roads, last thing we want is to get the pram wheels stuck in the tramcar rails."

The girls nodded but as yet made no move to start on the great expedition. Personal experience and even dire warnings from previous prampushers had taught them that Mistress MacRae always had one final admonition before wagons could eventually roll. As at last, at long last she waved them off at the close-mouth, Mima said: "And just don't let me hear of anyone ever calling ma son Drewie, Drew or any other such nonsence. His name is Andrew and if it's good enough for the Patron Saint of Scotland, then ma son also is called Andrew."

TWELVE

As the years of the depression with it shuttered shops, closed shipyards and mind-numbing poverty bit ever deeper into lives, the greater was the caring aspect in every tenement building. As Mima wrapped up in a cloth a sampling of her treacle-scones, she turned to young Lena and said: "Give these to yer Granny, hen, a wee tasty bite for her tea. And tell her ye did well with yer prampushing duties."

Lena gave a delighted grin. "Aye, Ah'll tell her right enough. Ma Granny aye says it'll be a sad day in Scotland when we cannae help each other, for we're all in this thegither."

Mima nodded. "Yer Granny's right enough, a real wise wee woman yer Granny."

As Mima hustled Lena out on her way back home before she would launch into a raft of every single one of her Granny's pet sayings, Mima's Mother called out from the bed: "A real nice wee lassie that, her Granny's bringing her up in the right way she should go."

Mima nodded her agreement. "Ah know Lena's Mother died in givin birth to her, but what aboot her Father, she never seems to see anything of him."

On hearing this, Sandy chipped in: "Oh him. He scuttled off to Australia soon as he'd got Nancy in the family way and the sound of fast-approaching wedding-bells was daein his heid in. Damn scunner of a man, probably got a wife or at least a bidie-in in every port and weans scattered the length and breadth of planet earth."

The words of Sandy's uncharacteristic outburst still hung in the air when Mima went across to him and smoothed back his grey hair.

"Uch, Sandy, it's me that's the lucky woman havin a guid man like yersell."

He pursed his lips, then mumbled: "Well, hen if ye think ye got a bargain wi a cripple like me for yer life's companion, then all Ah can say is this ... ye're gey easy pleased and then some."

Mima gasped. "That's a terrible thing tae say to me. And listen before ye start goin on again aboot ye no bringing in a penny piece into the household purse, Ah've got news for ye. Ah wasnae gonnae tell ye until Stoorie Sam would come in hissell tae tell ye aboot his grand idea, but whatever it is, he reckons it could be a big earner for the baith of youse. So there."

Sandy wore a puzzled frown. "Stoorie Sam? Ye mean yon wee bowlie-legged bachle that sells coal-briquettes roon the streets?"

Mima nodded. "The very man and a right decent wee hard hardworking, barra-pushin, trader he is."

Sandy shook his head in perplexity. "Decent or no. Ah just cannae imagine what kinda money-spinnin scheme he'd want tae involve me in. It's no even as if Ah could help him tae hurl his barra."

Mima tutted. "Hmph. Bow legs or no he's well able tae push his ain barra and trail his load o briquettes up-n-doon stairs on his own, thanks very much. And as tae what he wants tae discuss wi ye, ye'll just have tae be patient 'til the day and hour he chaps at oor door." Scarcely were the words out of her mouth than a rat-a-ta-tat-tat at the door caused them to start nervously.

But before Mima could open the door a voice called out: "It's only me Mistress MacRae, it's Angusina Kerr , ma Mammy says could ye come at once, she thinks wee Billy just swallowed a farthing."

Mima and her husband grinned at each other and Sandy said: "So much for thinkin a knock on the door heralded the arrival of Stoorie Sam and his fortune-making plans."

They laughed. "Talking of money," Mima said, "Ah'd better get upstairs to Mrs Kerr's, she'll be worrying herself sick if Ah know her."

Sandy called out after her "At least she has a farthing to her name and her precious fudgie isnae lost ... she kens where it is."

THIRTEEN

A few days later when Mima arrived home from one of her many wee jobs she found Sandy to be in a high good humour.

Sandy grinned. "Stoorie Sam's gonnae pay me good money for makin things that he can sell tae his briquette customers, did ye ever hear the likes?"

Mima could feel her eyes widen in utter amazement. "But what in the world could ye make? What have ye ever made that would bring us in guid money? Would ye just tell me that? The only thing ye've ever made, tae ma knowledge was yon wee spills and spillholders. Oh, here, ye don't mean ..."

Like a mischievous schoolboy Sandy grinned and nodded his head vigorously. "Got it in one Mima. And forbye, ye know yon firelighter thingies that Ah sometimes weave thegither anytime therr's an old newspaper kickin aboot the hoose."

Mima laughed "And many a battle we've had over that carryon, wi me wantin the old newspapers tae cut intae squares for the cludgie and ye tryin tae salvage enough pages for yer precious firelighters. Mind ye. Ah hae tae gae it tae ye, they certainly dae work, look how Mrs Tassie raved over the last couple Ah handed in tae her." There was a silence between them then Mima asked: "How do ye suppose Stoorie Sam heard o yer marvellous firelighters in the first place?"

Sandy settled himself more comfortably in his chair. "Nae mystery there, he mentioned some wee woman round in Cumberland Street, she's aye buyin his briquettes and she telt him aboot ..."

Mima clapped a scandalized hand to her mouth and the sudden action stopped her man in full flight. His own questioning look was answered only when Mima, having sufficiently recovered from the shock she'd just received, asked in hushed tones: "Ye don't mean tae say he actually mentioned her, had the bare-faced effrontery tae say that woman's name here in ma very ain hoose?"

Sandy, completely nonplussed at the way his triumphant tale of financial wheelings and dealings had somehow gone alarmingly off course, snapped back: "And why should Stoorie Sam no mention Hilda Strang? Seems she's his best customer."

Mima clenched her fists as if prepared to do battle. "Honestly, Sandy dae ye never listen tae any of the titbits of gossip Ah bring ye from ma work. See yon Hilda Strang, his best customer, ma Aunty Mary, there's a name for what she is ..."

"Who, yer Aunty Mary?"

"Sandy, wid ye pay attention tae what Ah'm tryin tae tell ye. and ma Aunty Mary's got nothin tae dae with it, honestly ye can be that thrawn at times.Ah'm talkin aboot that Hilda Strang. Therr's a name for what she is ... she's his fancy woman. There now, what dae ye make of that?"

Sandy threw his head back and roared with laughter.

When at last he could speak, he spluttered: "Ye're tellin me, yon bandie-leggit, shilpit wee man has actually got a fancy woman, beggars belief that does.If it is true, then bloody good luck tae the pair of them, but God help him if his wife, Battlin Beenie ever finds oot. Ye know if Ah had a drink in ma hands, Ah'd drink a toast tae the braveheart of Gorbals and his fancy woman."

Mima drew herself to her full height. "That's a scandalous thing tae say, scandalous, Ah'll not hear another word of such durty talk."

When it finally dawned on Mima that Stoorie Sam's extra-marital goings on had nothing whatsoever to do with a business relationship with her own guid man, she relaxed her own strict moral code. Even so, it was arranged that as and when the goods were ready for sale, it would be Sam's eldest boy, Gus, who would do the pickup and then later return with the amount of money realized from their sale.

On one such visit, the lad turned to Mima's Mother and more for the sake of making conversation to fill the uneasy silence, said: "Mrs

Reilly, ma Maw said tae tell ye she was fair delighted wi the shawl ye made for ma big sister's baby."

Bridget Reilly beamed happily. "Uch, that's good son, Ah'm glad she was pleased, it mibbe helped lighten family worries aboot clothin the poor faitherless bairn."

Gus looked down and toed patterns in the rag rug at his feet, then recovering sufficiently from his embarrassment said: "Ma Maw, she says in her opinion, instead of folk buyin ye the wool and then ye givin yer labour for nothin, ye could easily be selling crocheted shawls and stuff like that tae any Jenny-a-things shop."

Bridie smiled. "That's a real nice idea, Gus lad, but at ma time of life, Ah wouldnae want tae be working under pressure. This way Ah work tae ma ain speed and if folk are pleased enough tae hand me in the occasional medicine bottle of the water-o-life by way o a thank ye. That suits me just fine. Anyway there's somethin else yer Maw hasnae thought aboot in ma situation … Thanks tae yer Dad, Sandy's doing real well, clawin in the bawbees, and it gives him an interest as weel. Mima's a good wage-earner and now Andrew's getting older, even though by the law o the land he's no the right age for it, he's running aboot daft delivering milk, morning rolls and newspapers. So, with three folk in the hoose bringin in siller, why should Ah slave and work ma fingers tae the bone, when Ah don't need tae, just answer me that, son."

FOURTEEN

The year 1937 opened with the world-shaking news that one of Gorbals' own sons, Benny Lynch was now the undisputed Flyweight Champion of the World.

In an interview for The Daily Record, 'Little Benny, our own Benny' said: "Just now Ah feel proud Ah am a Scot and that Ah have kept the title for ma country."

Having defeated Small Montana of America on points over fifteen rounds, Lynch claimed two thousand, six hundred pounds of the six thousand pound purse. On arriving triumphant at Glasgow's Central Station, a day later, Benny was met by his close friend Tommy Morgan, the famous Scots comedian, who said: "We're all waitin to give ye a great welcome."

On reading this out to his Granny from the newspaper, young Andrew was then waxing fair about the many merits to be had, not least of which were untold riches, as a world-class boxer.

Still in full flight, Mima stopped him in his tracks. "Yes, all very wonderful Ah agree, who could ever imagine even one thousand pounds, never mind a fortune such as Benny now has ... But if ye harbour any ideas of ever becoming a celebrity boxer, get rid of them now. Yer Daddy, Granny and me all have much greater plans for ye. Meantime, content yersel with what ye have and count yersel lucky that the dairy and the newsagent have taken ye on, even though ye're mibbe still not the official age for such work. Now, be off with ye, ye cannae keep folk waiting for their morning milk, rolls and newspapers."

Later that very same week with Andrew having done his early morning milk and paper rounds and, having gone on his way to school, the three adults were sitting companionably over a fresh pot of tea. Having cleared her throat a few times, Bridget at last got out the words she had obviously been struggling to say: "Ah heard ye goin on at Andrew again this morning. Ye still bangin away at the drum that no son of yers would ever be a prizefighter. Oh no, A meenister of the Kirk, mair liker, that's what this mornin's sermon was all aboot.Weel, as tae that ..."

As her words faded away, Sandy prompted his Mother-in-law as with a decided twinkle in his eyes: "Aye, Granny, ye've got tae hand it tae oor Mima, delusions of grandeur right enough. Mind ye, the way she's been goin on at the lad recently, Ah thought she had it in mind for him tae be nothing lower than the Prime Minister of the country, never mind a sermon-spoutin Reverend Gentleman of the Kirk."

They all laughed then Bridie said: "Aye true enough, but that's no exactly what Ah'm tryin tae get at, ye see. Noo, how can Ah put this withoot upsetting the baith o youse and ..."

Mima tutted. "For heaven's sake, just spit it oot, Mother, whatever it is. We're no that easy knocked aff oor perch."

Her Mother raised her head high. "It's no ye two that would spend sleepless nights ower it, it's me. Ah'd be black-affrontit tae hae ma one and only grandson paradin the streets as a Scottish Kirkman o Religion ... me bein of the ither persuasion, if ye get ma meaning."

Mima and her husband exchanged glances, raised eyebrows telling their own story.

Finally Sandy waded in with both feet to the already sensitively fraught discussion.

"First time Ah've ever heard ye mention yer great interest in the two sides of the traditional religious divide, Granny. What's brung this on? For it'll be many a long day before Andrew's old enough tae leave the school never mind start donning a dog-collar and Kirk meenister's goonie."

Mima nodded. "Sandy's right , Ma, nae need for ye tae be worryin yer heid aboot such matters."

Bridie sat up straighter in bed, the decisive movement almost making a statement of its own, as she yet again cleared her throat. "Weel, Ah suppose this is as good a time as any tae clear the air, but Ah'm an auld woman, for heaven's sake, nearly seventy-one so Ah am and wi the best will in the world, naebody can last forever and so, Ah thought that ..."

Mima put out a restraining hand "Just stop right there, Ma, next thing ye'll be telling us what funeral hymns ye want and ye'll have me greetin like a wean."

Bridie, once started was clearly determined to go on, like it or lump it. "Ah think Ah'm what folk roonaboot here cry a lapped Catholic, or some such fancy name, or is it a collapsed Catholic?"

Sandy burst out laughing. "Uch, hen tell us somethin we don't already ken. Far as Ah can see, ye've been collapsed for years and that's the truth of the matter. Ah think the right phrase is a lapsed Catholic, but what has any o that tae dae wi ye, Granny, or with Andrew by some miracle becoming a sermon-spouting meenister. Cannae say Ah get the drift of any of this."

Bridget looked down her nose at him. "Ah thought ye were supposed tae be quick on the uptake, Sandy. Ye must be gey dumbfoonert if ye still cannae see what Ah'm driving at."

A silence fell in the room as each pursued independent lines of thought.

Finally Mima clapped the top of her head. "Ah get it. What ye really mean is this ... when ye're breathin yer last, knockin on Death's door and ye've had me running wi all ma legs to bring a crucifix-hingin, sins forgivin, last rites Catholic

Priest tae help ye on yer way tae the Pearly Gates, ye're no wantin him tae be competing wi yer Kirk Meenister grandson for the honour. Is that what this stramash is all aboot?"

Her Mother nodded causing Sandy to splutter: "Never heard the likes. Weel, Ah'm tellin ye noo, there'll be nae priests, nuns or any ither such incense-burnin carry-on in this hoose. And that's ma last word on the subject."

Mima glared at her husband, then she crossed the room to her Mother's bedside. With a trembling hand, Mima smoothed back her Mother's nest of flyaway white hair and said: "Listen, Mammy, God alone kens ye've never had much or asked much of this world's bounty for yersel. So, even if Ah gave up the Faith no long after ye did, if ye feel ye want to see a priest in yer last hours on earth tae ease yer passing intae the Great Beyond, then if Ah've tae move heaven and earth tae get him tae come, then a priest ye shall have."

Her Mother looked up through her trears. "Uch, ye're a real guid lass, Mima, that ye are. Ah've been blessed tae have a daughter like ye. Thank ye, and anyway, it's no even Sandy's house even though it's his name on the doorplate, so nuthin tae dae wi him. He forgets, if anybody's the ludger, it's him, he came tae stay wi us when ye and him got merrit."

Set in Her Ways

Mima frowned, uncertain how Sandy would take such straight talking. She was relieved when he gave a sheepish grin.

"Ah suppose that's me firmly put in ma place. Noo then, afore the pair o youse start chantin yer holy orders and hymn-singing like a Sally Ann prayer meeting, can we please just leave all this Holy Willie carry on? So we can get back tae whit passes for normal here, eh no?"

It was barely a month after what Sandy now referred to jokingly as, Yon Holy Willie bunfight, and more and more Bridget seemed to be living in the past. Increasingly she appeared to want young Andrew to know something of the family's history.

This became glaringly obvious when one day over breakfast porridge, he suddenly said: "Granny was tellin me that Ah've got two uncles livin out somewhere in Canada. No' that Ah'm ever likely tae meet them, but she seemed tae thing it important tae let me know of their existance."

Sandy looked up from contemplation of his own bowl of porridge "So that's what ye two were whisperin aboot the other night when Ah was trying hard to concentrate on fillin in ma football coupon."

Andrew grinned. "We wurnae exactly whisperin Daddy, But Granny's voice is that faint noo that Ah had tae bend ma head tae catch whit she was saying."

Mima stood over her son. "Yer Granny's an auld woman noo and therr's days she seems tae be livin in the past So just listen tae her tales, don't worry yersell, but if ever ye hear her chunterin on aboot Catholic Priests and the like, ye're tae tell me at once, d'ye hear?"

He nodded and Mima said: "Now get that porridge intae ye, for it's a gey cauld mornin oot there and ye need sumthin tae stick tae yer ribs."

"But Mammy, ye've never let dab that Ah have uncles anywhere, far less mibbe rich ones oot in Canada."

Mima playfully flapped a linen tea towel at his head. "Forget it, son, ye're never likely tae clap eyes on the hide nor hair of them, so just forget it."

Game to the last, he persisted: "But dae ye think mibbe Granny'll tell me more aboot ma uncles?"

Mima sighed. "Mibbe aye, mibbe hooch aye. But like Ah say, yer Granny's auld noo and some o the stuff she'll tell ye will just sound like Double-Dutch. So, put it oota yer heid, unless, of course, she starts on aboot the Chapel and a Priest, which could be very important to her."

Andrew appeared to consider this then said: "Is that a polite way of tellin me that the poor old soul's noo awa wi the fairies? Noo that she's auld and decrepit like."

Set in Her Ways

Mima laughed. "She'll soon give ye auld and decrepit if she hears ye saying such a thing. Right, that's it, Andrew, on yer way, sunshine, and don't forget tae wear that new muffler yer Granny knitted for ye, it'll help keep ye warm."

Andrew grinned. "It might keep me warm as toast all right, Mammy, but ma pals will laugh at me, it looks daft wi all the colours of the rainbow. D'ye no remember Granny used up all the odd bits of wool she had in her knitting bag?"

Mima and her husband exchanged smiles and Sandy said: "Tuck it inside yer jersey and a blind man runnin for his life widnae see it."

"Therr's mair than ma decayed auld mither sayin strange things," Mima said.

As Andrew went out the door. Sandy muttered: "At least so far Ah havnae made noises aboot askin for a Priest."

FIFTEEN

The month of February with its grim, miserable weather was fast drawing to a close and the one bright spot on the horizon was the prospect of something called the Empire Exhibition to be opened in Glasgow in the summer. There were rumours, counter-rumours and even wild theories being bandied about, and now here was Andrew going on about it.

"It's true Mammy and Miss Naismith, our teacher, she said if we can bring our threepence a week from now on, when the Empire Exhibition opens, she'll take us to visit it, for she says it's gonnae be a histroric event."

Mima considered this. "As to it goin intae the history books, Ah suppose yer teacher knows what she's talkin aboot. Aye, all right start payin in yer dues. We can spare that oota yer milk and paper rounds. But listen, never let dab tae yer teacher that ye're daein that work, for all Ah know ye're mibbe still too young by the Law of the Land and we're no wantin yon nosey wee Attendance Officer at the door tae chib us for ye sometimes being late intae the school."

"Uch, Mammy, ye've telt me all that areddies."

"Well, Ah'm tellin ye again, cheeky wee midden that ye are."

Andrew's face fell. "Ah wasnae meanin tae be cheeky, Mammy, but Ah'm no daft and there's a limit tae how many times ye can warn me aboot mibbe gettin clapped in Barlinnie Gaol for workin before the official age limit, whitever it should happen tae be."

Mima grinned. "If they bung ye intae the gaol, Ah'll bake ye a cake wi a file in it. But until then, for every threepence ye save at the school towards the Empire Exhibition outing, Ah'll get yer Daddy tae lay by another silver threepenny-bit in the guid wedding china teapot."

No sooner had their son left than Sandy said: "That was real kind of ye tae volunteer that Ah'd put thruppence a week towards his fund for the Empire Exhibition."

Mima grinned. "Ah knew ye widnae mind, especially noo that yer makin a fortune oota them firelighters and spillholders ye're selling by way of Stoorie Sam. Ye were saying just the ither day that ye're fair clawin in the bawbees, so dinnae try comin the skinflint wi me."

By and large, despite their occasional bickering Mima had to admit that marriage to her Sandy suited her well enough. If she were be be honest with herself, she had to admit that such marital rows as they had usually flared up when she was overtired from working at her early-morning cleaning job, bringing up her son, looking after her bedridden Mother and acting as nurse and helpmate for her bed-chair-bound husband's every need.

And of course, she thought, *not forgetting household shopping, cleaning cooking and stretching of every halfpenny to do the work of ten.*

In this, as in so many ways, Mima knew she was no different from the majority of other hard-pressed women, her near-neighbours who lived in the other single-ends, back-shops and room-and-kitchens.

Mibbe, come to think of it, just mibbe Ah'm a lot luckier than most of them ... the ones with a houseful of weans and a drunken husband lurching home legless on a Friday night with a near-as-dammit empty paypacket. Spewin his guts out, and demanding his marital rights. Marital rights. Hmph. Those poor women what rights of any kind, marital or otherwise, have they got? And then left with the worry indeed the absolute certainty of yet another mouth to feed in nine months' time.

Sandy's voice broke into her thoughts. "Mima, is that ye daydreaming again?"

She shook herself alert, approached his chair in its usual place by the fireside then reached out a hand and tousled his thinning hair.

"Uch Sandy, ye can read me like a book. If ye must know, Ah've just been thinkin how lucky Ah am , how very lucky tae have such a good man as yersel."

He smiled yet despite his obvious pleasure at such a compliment right out of the blue, still he clearly felt constrained to say: "Uch, Mima, hen, Ah've telt ye before, ye're easy pleased, that's all Ah can say. But listen, flattery will get ye everywhere. So come a wee bit closer and give us a cuddle and a wee cheeper. Ah'm just sorry that's the best Ah can dae. But for all that, fine weel ye know that Ah ..."

Mima gave a hasty nod. "Just leave it therr, Sandy don't ye dare go gettin all emotional on me, it's only filmstars, gentry and high-fallutin folk like that, that can afford the time and luxury of spoutin aboot undying love. That's no for the likes of us."

The raw emotion of the moment now firmly deflated. Sandy, clearly glad to be back on safer ground, grinned. "Heark tae ye. And what exactly would yer ladyship know of such high-born, high-livin folk? Film stars indeed. Ah never heard the likes of it in all ma born days."

Mima looked down at him and with a giggle in her voice and she was sure with a twinkle in her eyes, said: "Ye know, Sandy, for a reasonably intelligent man, ye can be gey stupid at times. Ye're forgettin ma wee cleanin job at the Majestic. What wi posters, adverts for their films and pictures o glamorous women and handsome dinner-jacketed men, Ah'm mixin wi film stars every day of ma life. So, there. Put that in yer pipe and smoke it."

Mima was still clearing away the breakfast things when Andrew, blue with cold from his milk-round, arrived.

Blowing on his hands, he smiled up at her. "Mammy, any chance of a hot cup of tea and a jeelie-piece before Ah head off tae school?" He held out a paper bag. "Big Ettie at the dairy, she said tae gie ye these rolls, they're mibbe a wee bit stale, but she said they'll be all right for toastin at the fire."

As she took the poke of rolls from him, Mima said: "Ah jist hope ye havenae been lettin on tae Ettie that Ah'm starvin ye. Ah'd be black affrontit if the word on the street was that we hadnae got enough tae eat."

Sandy called over: "Mima hen, ye worry too much. We're all the same here in the Gorbals, fine weel ye know we help each other, so jist be grateful for the rolls and for goodness sake feed that poor starvin laddie of ours."

Some time later, battered schoolbag on his back and another jeelie-piece clutched in one hand, Andrew turned at the door to say: "Ah've telt Big Ettie that Ah'll dae a morning's work as well as ma milk round every Saturday from now on. Ever since yon handyman friend of hers hanged hissel from a tree in Glesga Green, well, withoot havin him tae lend a hand in the back shop of the Dairy, she's needin extra help in shiftin boxes and ither heavy stuff like that."

Set in Her Ways

Mima raised her eyebrows. "That's all very well and Ah'm heartfelt sorry for her that she lost her guid friend tae such a tragic death, and by the way, Ah think ye should be showin the poor soul a bit of respect, her name is Ethel, even though most folk roonaboot here cry her Big Ettie. Disnae sound right when she's suffering a bereavement, noo does it?"

Andrew made another attempt to leave and muttered: "But whit aboot the idea of me working an extra shift on Saturdays, is that an aye or a no, Mammy?"

Mima demurred. "Jist one thing bothers me, Ah thought ye liked gettin back tae yer bed on a Saturday mornin? Ye surely don't feel obliged tae dae extra work, heavy liftin and all, jist the sake of the occasional bag of stale rolls?"

Andrew laughed and patted the side of his nose, in a knowing gesture. "Ah'm no daft, Mammy, nae comin up the Clyde on a water biscuit for me. Naw, naw, She's agreed tae pay me time and a half."

Mima frowned. "She must be real desperate for yer help, that's all Ah can say."

He grinned. "Uch, fine well she kens Ah'm tryin hard for tae save some money for that big exhibition they keep talkin aboot that they're supposed tae be having in Bellahouston Park this year. And Big ... er Ethel, she's a real decent wee woman, she says she'd as soon any extra money that's going aboot should go tae me."

Mima patted his hand. "Good for ye son, ye're a hard worker, Ah'll say that for ye, but jist don't get tae thinkin that money is the be-all-and-end-all o life."

With one foot out the door, he leant in and with a cheeky grin said: "Funny that, for ma Dad aye says that a handful o thrupenny bits in yer pocket is yer best friend, that no right Dad?"

Sandy laughed. "Ah'll let ye and yer Mother argue it out atween the pair of youse. Anyway, is it no high time ye were at the school, at this rate ye're gonnae be late."

Andrew nodded. "Oh help ma boab, would ye look at the time. Right, school here Ah come. For Ah'm no right educated yet and Ah need all the learnin Ah can get."

As she gave him a playful shove to help him on his way, Mima laughed. "Seems tae me ye could be learnin yer teachers a thing or two whether ye're the right age or no for work, here's ye a schoolboy wi nae less than three payin jobs, and some trained teachers nooadays cannae get a job of ony kind for love nor money."

As the door crashed shut behind him Sandy grinned at Mima. "A bright lad that, he'll go far. Must get his brains from ma side o the family."

Mima threw a crumpled-up dishcloth at her grinning husband.

SIXTEEN

The early days, weeks and months of the year 1938 ground slowly on, seemingly endlessly until at last, the long-awaited grand opening of the Empire Exhibition arrived. On the day of his visit to Bellahouston Park, if Andrew was in a state of high excitement before he left, that was as nothing compared to his euphoria on his return.

"Mammy," he started the minute he came in, "Mammy, Ye've never saw nuthin like it ... the Tait's Tower, the coloured waterfalls, the Grand Staircase, the Highland Clachan, that's a real village wi real Hielan crofters sittin at their doorways cardin and spinnin wool. And then there's the Amusement Park with even a haunted house and roundabouts like wee flying machines and there's something sweet called candy-floss and toffee apples on wee bits of stick and there's giraffe-necked women wi rings of metal roon their thrapples and the Palace of Engineering. Best of all there's Canada House wi real red-uniformed Mounties guardin it. Oh Mammy. Talk aboot the wonders o the world all up yonder at Bellahouston. Can ye imagine it, all here in Glasgow."

When at last her son stopped for breath Mima burst out laughing. "Wonders of the world indeed. And by the sound of it ye must have saw every last one of them in this single visit. Well seen ye enjoyed yer class outin, that was awful good of yer teacher takin a crowd of weans, anyway the ones that had paid up their money every week."

He nodded. "Aye, worth every halfpenny, so it was."

Mima smiled. "Ah think Ah got that message loud and clear, son. And thanks for describing it all for me, son, for that's the nearest Ah'll ever get tae any single bit of the Exhibition."

As her words faded away, Mima could not hold back a feeling of sadness.

Hmph, she thought, *the whole of Glasgow in high carnival spirit aboot all these marvels from around the world and what have Ah got out of it?*

She gazed into the far distance at a point only she could see.

What was it the manager of the Majestic said tae me? Oh aye, 'Sorry but Ah cannae afford yer valuable cleaning services any more. The way Ah see it, Mima, is this, folks roonaboot here will be spendin whatever money they can lay their hands on up at yon Exhibition ... and that means ma takings here at the Majestic will be goin doon the drain. Stands tae reason, doesn't it?'

Mima had begged him to keep her on at her job, suggesting: "Mibbe less hours a week or even a wee reduction in pay until things get back to normal once the Empire Exhibition shuts?"

While Mr Taylor had appeared to consider such a solution, finally, with a decidedly embarrassed look on his face, he came out with the real truth of the matter.

"Mima, if ye must know and ye've worked long enough and hard enough here over the years no tae be fobbed off with a half-truth."

As Mima had stood wringing her hands in an agony of despair, finally Mr Taylor said: "The thing is it's ma granddaughter, she's Exhibition-daft like all the rest of the young folk and she's wantin tae earn a wee bit pocket money to save up for it. So, if Ah pay her even half of what ye're getting, that's everybody happy."

Everybody happy, indeed everybody except me, Mima had thought.

As a last ditch attempt to salvage her job, or at the very least something from the ruins of her once-prized job she said: "Mr Taylor, sir, what about later on once the Exhibition is over and done with and just a memory? Could ye mibbe take me back then?"

The picture house manager, a decent enough boss in the normal way, shook his head, looking decidedly shamefaced about the whole business.

"Sorry, Mima, but Ah've promised to keep Isabel on even then ... she said if Ah helped her get money for the Exhibition, later on she'd work for me for nothing, she's that desperate. And forbye, with times being hard for me, it was an offer Ah jist couldnae refuse. After all, she is ma granddaughter, and a promise is a promise."

Mima thought. Ah jist hope she'll keep her side of the bargain when the time comes.

Mima still standing lost in gloomy contemplation of her lost and now gone forever job at the Picture Palace, suddenly shook herself free of her reverie when she heard a voice at her elbow say, "Mammy. Ye were miles away there, did ye no hear what Daddy and me was sayin tae ye, what we've been tryin tae tell ye for the past ten minutes?"

Mima shook her head and assuming what she hoped was a sufficiently interested look in whatever had been going on, she hastened to say: "Sorry, son, but Ah was jist that blown away in ma mind by all the wonders of the world that ye described tae me. Ah was tryin ma best tae see it in ma mind's eye but for the life of me, Ah jist cannae imagine what a giraffe-necked woman could possibly look like. Ah mean tae say, Andrew, therr's many a strange lookin character here in the Gorbals but we're a wee bit thin on the ground as far as women wi brass rings roonaboot their thrapples."

Andrew threw back his head and laughed. "Forget yer mind's eye mammy, ye're really gonnae see them steel-necked women and everything else."

Before Mima could make a reply of any kind, Sandy, sitting up straighter in his bedchair, said: "Andrew's right, hen. Lissen. Ye're no oot the way of needin a wee bit treat, so between what Andrew has left from his spending money and ..."

Mima turned to face her son. "But, Andrew, ye bought me that souvenir hanky, a maple-leaf design ye said: edged with lace and all, that must have cost ye a pretty penny."

Her son's face coloured a painful beetroot-red. "If ye must know, Mammy, that didnae cost me as much as a farthin, not one single fudgie. One of the workers in the Canadian Pavilion gave it tae me for free."

Mima frowned. "And why exactly would any stranger dae that?"

Andrew grinned. "We got talkin and Ah said that accordin tae ma Granny Ah'm supposed tae hae two uncles in Canada. and the man said: 'Well, in that case, if ye've got links with my country, please take this souvenir hanky to yer Granny or yer Mother. My own Granny told me that Scottish Grannies and Mothers are the salt of the earth. It's the first time Ah've been here, so please take this with my best wishes, least Ah can do.'"

Mima could feel tears of emotion well up in her eyes and seeing this Sandy said: "Haud on a meenit, Mima, before ye start moppin at yer greetin face wi that swanky wee lace-edged hanky, could ye at least let me finish whit Ah was tryin tae tell ye."

Mima squared her shoulders. "Nobody stoppin ye as far as Ah can see, Sandy MacRae."

Jenny Telfer Chaplin

He made a funny face at her then went on, "As Ah was sayin when Ah was so rudely interrupted, Ah'll pitch in some of ma tobacco money and between that and Andrew's contribution the pair of youse can spend next Saturday up at the precious Exhibition."

Mima's face and exclamation of delighted astonishment said it all.

But even before she could speak her Mother called out from the wall-bed, "And if ye're bringin me an Exhibition souvenir, ye can forget any free-handoot hankies, ma mind is set on a toffee-apple, an apple drookit in toffee and speared onto a stick; whatever will they think of next?"

Sandy said: "Ah don't know that's such a novelty, surely they had toffee-apples when ye were a wean Granny?"

Quick as a flash Granny replied, "Uch, Ah'm an auld woman, Ah cannae mind that far back noo. Onyway, Ah've never had one from ony Canadian Pavilion before and forbye, Andrew, ye mentioned something aboot them being dipped in maple syrup, whatever that might be."

Sandy got the last laugh in when he said: "Right, auld yin, a toffee-apple it shall be, jist as long as ye think yer auld gnashers can take the strain of chompin yer way through the trunk of a Canadian maple-tree. Tell ye one thing, it wouldnae be ma cup of tea."

Bridget called back: "See ye, Sandy MacRae, ye're a cheeky wee midden so ye are, ma auld

90

gnashers isnae none o yer business. Onyway, who ever said that a cup of tea was yer favourite tipple. That's no the way Ah've heard it."

As their shared laughter died away, Mima was left with the feeling that having lost her job at the Majestic or not, even so, she was hugely blessed. She had a fine upstanding son, a Mother who loved her and who despite recent health scares and talk of Last Rites and a hoped-for Priest, nevertheless was still in the land of the living. She also had a good man of her own who although confined to a chairbed for the rest of his life, worshipped the very ground on which she walked.

Who could ask for anything more? Mima wondered, *Was there any other Gorbals housewife who had such a rich store of life's blessings?*

SEVENTEEN

When, in the course of time, Mima and her son came back from their gala Saturday visit to the Empire Exhibition, while yet again Andrew was loud in his praise of the many wonders he had seen, Mima on the other hand was fully aware that she herself was being strangely reticent in discussing anything at all about their visit.

Later that Saturday evening with her son in his hurlie-bed and his Granny in the wall bed she shared with Mima, Sandy laid a hand on Mima's arm. "Right, ma lass, what ails ye? Ah'd remind ye that, as ye've so often said yersel, Ah can read ye like a book. So, come on now, out with it, tell yer Sandy. Was it seeing all those wonders ye suddenly realized what a pitiful existence ye yersel have here? Ah mean tae say, fine weel Ah know the last straw must surely have been when ye lost yer wee job at the Picture Hoose, for it means ye'll hae tae stretch the money even further noo."

Mima sighed. "It's no even as simple as that. Lissen, Sandy, what Ah've done this day, ye're bound tae think it a very foolish thing."

Sandy shook his head in instant disbelief. "Weel, ye didnae elope wi one o those braw Canadian Mounties that Andrew's forever goin on aboot. Ye, doin something foolish? Ye havenae a stupid or unkind bone in yer body. Ye're ma ain dear wee wifie And see me, Mima, Ah'm the lucky man that knows it."

Mima laid a hand on his. "Sandy, please, jist hear me oot, if Ah don't tell ye soon, Ah'll burst. The stupid thing Ah done, only went and gave ma mother's name and address tae a complete stranger o a Mountie."

"Have Ah got the second sight or what? Telt ye there was a Mountie involved somewhere, didn't Ah? Anyway, cannae see much harm in tellin folk where we live. It's no as if it's a big state secret or nuthin."

Over a late-night cup of cocoa, the sorry tale was told with all its twists, turns and vivid imaginings until at last having grasped all the details from the rambling account, Sandy a note of wonderment in his voice recapped: "So, the other two that ye havenae even seen yet, twin brothers ye say, they were away wandering the streets of Glasgow in the vain hope of somehow finding their Scottish kith and kin. So here's ye thinkin they might be yer brothers, yer long-lost brothers, Uch, come on, hen, how far-fetched is that?"

Mima chewed at her lower lip. "From what the other chap Ah spoke to said. the two heritage seekers, they're twins, born and worked in the Gorbals, left for a new life in Canada after some sort of works accident. And then lost all touch with their home folk in Scotland."

Sandy pursed his lips. "Ah can see what's got ye goin on this, all the bits fit thegither, at least from what ye yersel know of yer family's past history and from what ye've told me over the years, no forgetting that ye were a baby when they left for a new life in Canada. Here, haud on a meenit, where's ma brains been, there's an easy answer to this ... something that will clinch the matter in a wanny. What's their surname?"

Mima frowned. "The man Ah spoke to knew them only by their nicknames, Jock and Jimmy, and jist heard aboot their heritage search from somebody else. He didnae even know their surnames, or if he did, he wasnae for tellin me. He mibbe didnae want tae raise anybody's hopes unduly and Ah can understand that, so that's why Ah gave this other chap the name and address of Mrs Bridget Reilly, to pass on to them if the occasion arose and then the rest would be up to them."

Sandy nodded. "Like Ah say, not one bit of harm in that, hen, so what is it that's really bothering ye?"

Mima gave a heartfelt sigh. "Suppose they do choose to follow it up, come knockin at oor door, what kinda shock would that be for ma auld Mother? We had enough of a panic with that last false alarm when she was within an ace of havin me runnin with all ma legs for the Priest."

Sandy cast a surreptitious glance over to the huddled figure in the wallbed. "Sh, hen. better

keep yer voice doon or she'll hear every word.
Times Ah think she's no as deaf or even as daft as
she makes oot tae be."

Sandy as if officially bringing their discussion
to an end, with a decided air of finality said:
"That's it, enough for one night and nothing more
to be done about any of it. It may never happen.
They abandoned her, right? So most likely
outcome of all this stramash, a Christmas Card
from across the seas and if she's lucky a wee
packet of maple-leaf decorated hankies. Noo then,
Mima hen, can we let it rest there? Ah'm dead beat
wi all this. High time ye were in yer bed anyway,
ye've had an exciting day. Mind ye, there cannae
be all that many Exhibition goers who instead of
gitterin on aboot the wonders of the world, come
back wi all the worries of the world on their
shoulders. Just forget it, hen."

EIGHTEEN

Next day, Mima's Mother crooking her forefinger, silently beckoned her daughter over to her bedside. "What was all that whisperin that was goin on last night? Ah could only catch bits of it. Somethin aboot not wantin tae give me too much of a shock. And something aboot long-lost relatives. As far as Ah'm concerned, any that are lost, can stay lost. Any bastard that abandoned me in ma hour o need, they neednae think they can ever come saunterin back intae ma life for the big welcome hame. Dae ye get ma meanin, Mima?"

Her daughter nodded. "Seems tae me yer hearing's improved if ye managed tae get all that information from an overheard conversation."

Her Mother tapped the side of her nose. "Ah heard enough tae know that Ah want nae truck wi any digging up the past. No, at this time in ma life, all Ah'm wantin is a bit of peace. And when ma time is near, as Ah've already telt ye, some spiritual comfort from the St. Francis Chapel Priest. Surprises, shocks, folks dug up from the past ... Ah'm no needin ony of that. Dae ye understand me?"

Mima smiled. "Ah think Ah get yer meanin, but before ye start on again aboot yer funeral hymns, jist let me get this perfectly straight in ma mind, for Ah wouldnae want ye comin back frae the Land-o-the-Leal tae haunt me, for no obeyin yer last wishes tae the letter of the law."

Bridget Reilly said. "Ah want nuthin new, different or in any way ower exciting tae upset ma candy-barra. Ah'm weel content wi ma life the way it is right this very meenit. Ah'm truly blessed living here with ye, young Andrew and, of course, yer guid man Sandy."

Mima laughed. "Oh ye've changed yer tune. Ah still mind when ye used tae call him that Postie Fella."

Sandy stirred. "Somebody takin ma name in vain? Honestly no a minute's peace tae be had here."

Mima went across and laid a hand on his shoulder. "Funny that, ma Mother was jist sayin the very opposite. The way she tells it we're all living in some kinda Paradise, living the Gorbals' dream. In fact, she disnae want us tae change a thing in her ideal life."

Sandy swivelled round his head. "Aye, she's aw there, yer auld Mother, like me, she keeps tae the age-auld rule of living ... if a thing isnae broke, don't fix it." He gave Mima a meaningful wink, "Noo, is it all right wi ye two bletherin women if Ah can get back tae ma afternoon nap, fair enjoyin it so Ah was."

Nothing more was said on the subject of the family-tree seekers until one day Sandy mentioned:

"Funny how that business all jist fizzled out, never heard aboot it ever again."

At these words, Mima could feel the hot colour rush into her cheeks. To hide her embarrassment, she kept her head bent down and scrubbed harder than was necessary at the wooden breadboard. She mumbled a non-committal reply and her husband convinced that the upsetting carry-on was now over and done with, returned to his perusal of his daily newspaper.

Mima dried off the scrubbed-to-an-inch- of-its-life breadboard, then busy with essential household chores, she knew that nothing could or would halt the train of thought then surging through her brain. The soul of honesty, it still rankled with her that in withholding details of her own part in the potential domestic drama, she was being less than truthful with her husband. With regard to her Mother, however, who had declared quite categorically that she wanted nothing new brought in to trouble her at her time of life, feelings of guilt just did not enter.

Sandy called over. "Is there mibbe a wee cup of tea going, hen?"

Mima raised her head. "Now there's a guid idea, tell ye what, give me a minute tae run doon tae the the City Bakeries and Ah'll get us all a wee treat."

Not one to be left out of any such conversation or proposal, Bridget then spoke up.

"That's great, Mima, could ye make mine a chocolate eclair. Ah could jist go that."

Sandy laughed. "Keep on like this, a body would think we're celebratin somethin."

Mima wiped her hands, shrugged herself into her coat, then turning at the door said: "See ma Mother, according to her she celebrates every day spent here in oor company in oor wee Gorbals palace. Anyway, Sandy, what are ye ... a pineapple tart?" Her husband roared with laughter. "Ah've been called many a thing in ma life but never before a pineapple tart. Ye could get a wheen of different meanings out of that label. And whit aboot Granny there, wi all her recent talk aboot Priests and such. Think aboot it, the label might be mair suited tae her than tae me."

Bridget at once caught his meaning and scowled. "That's no a polite thing tae say. Ah know that some o youse Proddies call the Chapel a pineapple." Then, she laughed and she was cackling with laughter as Mima went out the door.

As she reached the communal close, Mima knocked on the door of Mrs Vernon, otherwise known to all and sundry as 'The Queen of the Close'. Nobody came in or went out of this particular close but what Mrs Vernon knew of it; she it was who chased marauding children, urinating drunks, and officious, even menacing debt-collectors; she it was who took it upon herself to ensure that every housewife took her rightful turn of washing the stairs, not forgetting to execute with precision the ornate pipe-clay edging. Had she wanted to speak with any other of her immediate neighbours, then in the time-honoured way, Mima would have rattled the requisite brass letterbox, opened the door and yelled, "yoo- hoo, it's only me." But in dealing with Mrs Vernon, regal to her fingertips, one had to be much more circumspect and a definite decorum strictly adhered to. So, when having knocked on the door, not having dared touch the gleaming brass bellpull, and the door opened to reveal the regal personage, Mima at once said: "Is it all right if Ah come in for a minute, Mistress Vernon?" The other woman nodded and once inside gleaming wee palace which reeked of vinegar and furniture polish, Mima said: "Ah jist wanted to double-check ... those men Ah mentioned that ma Mother had no wish to see, Ah take it they never came back?"

Mrs Vernon waved Mima to a chair. "As a matter of fact, they did return, still looking for a Mrs Reilly and seemingly convinced they had the right address. Ah had to come the strong madam with them. Listen, says Ah, check out all the nameplates for yerselves if ye don't believe me. The only Irish names are Cassidy, a Docherty, and a Monaghan."

Mima gave a sigh of relief. "Ah'll never be able to thank ye enough, Mrs Vernon, after all it was only the briefest of details Ah gave ye."

Set in Her Ways

The Queen nodded. "Ye told me yer Mother was hiding from these two men. That was good enough for me. None of ma business to ask who or what they were ... debt-collectors, illegitimate sons, or even Jehovah's Witnesses, all the same to me."

Mima had to rein in an involuntary smile at the classification of possible visitors, then the other woman went on: "One thing's for sure, they will not be back, Ah sent them off with a flea in their ear."

Mima rose to her feet. "Well, thanks again. By the way, we're having a wee treat from the City Bakeries, so can Ah hand in yer favourite cake? Ah would ask ye to join us for a cup of tea, but Ah know ye never like to leave yer window."

The keeper of the lookout post nodded, in total acceptance of her known role in the community. "Aye, Ah hardly ever desert ma post, that's the way we can keep our close so clean, tidy and above all, respectable. Anyway, ye were asking about ma favourite cake. Well Ah'm a cream sponge, or failing that mibbe a flies' cemetery, thank ye kindly."

As Mima walked along the street she smiled at the thought: *Ah don't know that Ah see Mrs Vernon as anything so soft as a cream sponge and anything less like a flies' cemetery Ah've never met. No, Ah've got it ... as Queen of all she surveys, defender of the good, the clean , the upright, Ah see her more as an Empire Biscuit. Aye, that's it, an Empire Biscuit, the very dab. But she did ask for a cream sponge, so if it's in ma power, then her every wish shall be granted ... and mibbe Ah could even curtsey when Ah go back.*

NINETEEN

As Andrew supped his porridge early one morning, Mima said: "Now listen, Andrew, January can be a real treacherous month what with snow, fog and icy roads and pavements, so heed what Ah'm tellin ye and jist ye be extra careful when yer out doing yer deliveries on a morning like this. Do ye understand what the dangers are?"

Her son looked up, an impish smile on his face. "Dangers, ye say, Mammy? Oh aye, fine weel Ah know all aboot them: Let's see noo, even last week, the newspapers said it was the worst fog for years, folk got drowned when they fell inae the Clyde in the pea-souper; buses, lorries and tramcars all crashing aboot intae each other. And even ships colliding oot in the river. Ye couldnae see yer finger in front of ye, no wonder they cried it 'Black Tuesday' Is that mibbe the kinda danger ye're gitterin on aboot, Mammy? Mind ye, trust me. Ah got back safe enough, in the one piece from ma milk round did Ah no? Ye must admit that."

Mima gave a mock frown. "Aye, aye, but there's nae call for ye tae get all smart and cocky wi me. Ye might think ye're a big man but a wee shirt still fits ye. So jist ye be careful ma lad, don't forget ye're jist ma wee boy."

He shook himself free of her impulsive embrace. "Uch, Mammy, Ah'm no a baby, Ah'll be ten come September, Ah'm gettin tae be too auld for cuddles."

Mima laughed. "Ah'll remind ye of that once ye're a young man busy at the winchin o some good-lookin wee lassie. Anyway, enough chatter, better get yer skates on, big man, or at this rate ye'll be late."

"One minute ye're tellin me tae be careful, next thing Ah'm supposed tae skate oota here at high speed on tae icy pavements. Which is it tae be, Mammy? For clever as ye say Ah am, Ah cannae dae the baith things at the one time."

She made a playful swipe at him with the dishcloth. "Clever, indeed? Mair liker a cheeky wee midden. Get oota this hoose right now. Jist a good job for ye that yer Daddy's sleeping and yer dotin Granny's feigning sleep tae pretend she cannae hear such cheek. The very idea, talking back tae me." As her son turned to make good his escape, Mima warned "And don't bang the door on yer way oot, yer Daddy needs all the sleep he can get."

As the door crashed shut behind him and its sound echoed in the room Sandy stirred in his chairbed.

"Ah knew it, told him, so Ah did. Told him not to waken ye up, if it could be helped. But oh no, what does yer son and heir do, only bang the door shut behind him, that's all."

Her husband shook his head. "If ye must know, Mima, Ah wisnae really sleepin, jist lyin here quietly, daein naedbody ony harm and listenin tae the pair o youse jabberin and snipin awa at each other."

Mima frowned. "Now don't ye start, Sandy MacRae, bad enough wi the one."

Her husband eased himself up in his chairbed. "Lissen, hen, ye'll need tae make up yer mind and quick aboot it, is he still yer wee baby or are ye brave enough tae give him the freedom tae become his ain man? For like it or lump it, oor Andrew has spirit, and wi gumption like that, next thing before ye realise it, he'll jump at adventure, run off tae sea or join the sojers as a drummer boy."

Mima's face clouded and she rounded on him. "Ye're his Father, but Ah don't see ye doin ower much tae train him in the way he should go."

TWENTY

1939

Ever since his visits to the Canadian Pavilion at the Empire Exhibition, young Andrew had been captivated by the romantic image of a wonderful far-off country peopled entirely by impressively-uniformed Mounties surrounded on all sides by mountains of pancakes. His enthusiasm rose to such heights that with even the slightest encouragement, he would declaim to any captive audience, "Yes, once Ah'm old enough to emigrate, then Canada's the country for me. Who knows, one day, Ah might even become a Mountie, red uniform, stately horse, syrup pancake breakfasts, the lot."

As September 1939 drew ever closer, many were the arrangements already being discussed and formulated to evacuate children from the industrial cities to places of supposed safety out in the country. On being made aware of this and precisely what his own school authorities were planning, the normally easygoing Andrew really dug his heels in.

"Mammy, Ah'm goin tae nae pig farm oot in the wilds of Ayrshire or Lanarkshire. No, this is where Ah stay. where Ah belong, here in Glasgow.

Where Ah've got ma milk and newspaper rounds; where ma pals are. No, they'll no move me oota the Gorbals."

When Mima started to protest that as a child, he'd do as he was told, he suddenly gave an impish grin. "Unless, of course, ye'd let me go to Canada. As ye know it's the one place Ah'd really love to live in and make a future."

His Mother broke in to have the last word. "Andrew, despite what ye seem to think, surely to goodness the entire country o Canada cannae really be stappit fu of brave red-coated Mounties, all sookin away at toffee-apples. And before ye start on again aboot yer so-called, long-lost uncles in the Prairies ... ye know that was all a lot of yer Granny's bletherins, please, can we just give it a rest?"

Although nothing more was said on the subject, Andrew's body language told its own story and this was apparent as he shuffled out the door, schoolbag slung carelessly across bowed shoulders.

Mima's husband turned to her and said: "Ah think mibbe ye were a wee bit hard on the laddie there, hen. Crushin all his dreams in a wannie. Ah could be wrong, but Ah think he still goes on that much aboot Canada as it helps tae take his mind off the sight of his poor auld Granny hirplin doon the brae at such high speed. He doesnae mention it much, or put his feelings intae words, but he worries himself sore aboot his Granny. Ah've seen

107

the way he watches her as if at times he can hardly believe she's still here in the land of the livin."

Mima could feel her eyes widen in surprise. "Didnae know ye were such an observer of the domestic scene, Sandy. In that case, ye'll have realised that he's no the only one tae be worried aboot Granny, she seems get mair frail and decrepit every day that passes. But if as ye say, talkin and thinkin aboot Canada helps Andrew, well, Ah suppose that can only be for the best tae stop him worrying ower much."

Nothing more was said between Mima and her man on the taboo subject, until one morning a few weeks later. As he read his copy of the Daily Record propped up as usual against the sugar basin on the oilcloth-covered breakfast table, Sandy suddenly let out a shout, spluttered, nearly choked over his porridge and finally said: "Listen tae this, Mima. Honestly, ye're never gonnae believe this."

Mima stopped, dishcloth in hand. "Well, Ah'll certainly not believe it unless ye tell me what ye're on about, now will Ah?"

"They're sending children at risk of the war over to America, South Africa and Canada to escape the threat of bombs in our country."

"Well, we'd better not let Andrew read that, or he'll not give us a minute's peace until he's on the high seas, outward-bound on the next ship sailing to Canada."

Set in Her Ways

Her husband nodded. "Aye, Ah see what ye mean. But uch, hen, nae need tae worry yer heid aboot it. It says here in the newspaper that these children are tae be privately evacuated tae guest homes out there. So, we've nae relatives oot in Canada …" he gave her a meaningful look, "… nae relatives tae act as guest-homes, and there's fare money involved. Ah doubt if his milk round wages would run tae that expense. So that lets Andrew out at the very first hurdle."

Mima frowned, chewed on her lower lip. "Mm. Even so, we both ken oor Andrew can be a real determined wee character once he's made up his mind tae something. Best thing tae dae is, use that newspaper for some of yer firelighters for Stoorie Sam. It'll be oota harm's way then, especially since neither wan of us will be letting dab aboot any such overseas evacuation scheme. Right, get busy weaving some of yon special firelighters and dae it noo."

TWENTY ONE

On Friday, 6th September, 1940, the Daily Record in accordance with wartime's strict censorship regulations, reported:

CHILDREN'S LINER SAVED – TOWED INTO NORTH BRITISH PORT.

This was accompanied by a picture of some children arriving in Scotland, now safe from their hideous ordeal of having had their evacuee ship torpedoed. Censorship rules or not, rumours in and around the Clyde, soon established that the North British Port was none other than Greenock. When outward bound to Canada, amazingly every single one of the 320 evacuee children had been miraculously saved from a watery grave. Despite his Father's best efforts, somehow Andrew managed to follow every twist and turn of the story.

"He must read the papers as he delivers them," said Sandy. 'So much for me working the night shift making firelighters tae keep the news from him."

A couple of weeks later, when suitably rested and refreshed from their recent ordeal , the group of children set out again for yet another stab at evacuation to Canada. On hearing of this latest development, Andrew went on and on about the fact that had it been in his power: "Ah'd have been going on that boat with them. Lucky things, now they're heading full-steam ahead for a new life in Canada. Lucky old them."

Finally, one day when she could stand his harping on about it not one minute longer, his Mother said: "All right, so they were indeed fortunate, blessed even, to escape with their lives the first time, Ah'll grant ye that. But who's to say that their next ship will be any safer from enemy attack? There is still a war raging and lightning can strike twice in the one place ye know."

Even as she said these words, Mima shivered as she ushered her son out on his way to school and a draught of cold air from the communal close beyond caught her unawares.

As she cleared away the breakfast things, again she shivered and Sandy called over. "Are ye all right, hen? Ye're lookin a wee bit peelie-wallie."

Mima felt that somehow her words had come aback to haunt her when only weeks later another cryptic, terse newspaper report mentioned that 'Due to enemy action seventy-seven evacuee children had been drowned in the North Atlantic. Of the forty-six children who survived a horrendous eight-day lifeboat ordeal, yet again they were brought safely back to a North British Port.'

A photograph showed their arrival many still wearing their school trench coats, to which were still attached rather crumpled-looking identification labels. Other children wrapped up in blanket-shawls were wearing carpet slippers and some of the younger girls were clutching, as to a lifeline, somewhat damp, droopy baby-dolls. Once this picture appeared in print, it was hardly surprising that everywhere these little survivors of the horrors of war went, they were feted and cheered in the streets as being akin to war heroes returning from a battle front.

When word reached Glasgow Councillors that a number of these brave young survivors, bemused yet delighted yet again to be safely back in Bonnie Scotland had expressed a desire to wear the kilt, then warmhearted, outgoing as ever, Glasgow, in the guise of fairy godmother, granted their every wish.

Arriving breathless, decidedly out of puff between rushing and undue excitement Andrew dashed into his home to say, "Mammy, would ye believe it, not only are they tae be fitted out with kilts, sporrans, Glengarries and even silver buckles, but after a photo-session to show off their new outfits, they're being treated to their tea with the Lord Provost, Patrick Dollan himself, at the City Chambers, isn't that wonderful?"

Sandy looked up from his newspaper. "Aye, hen, it's all true, Andrew's got the news every bit as good as ma Daily Record here. And would ye jist know it ... trust guid auld generous-tae-a fault Glesga tae come up trumps. They cannae afford tae mend the pavements, but they can aye dig deep intae the Civic Purse for a humanitarian gesture like this, and one that the whole world will soon know aboot. Typical. Trust oor toon cooncillors tae polish up their ain image while they're at it."

Mima frowned and pointed an admonitory, housewifely forefinger. "Sandy MacRae, Ah'm ashamed of ye. Ye're surely not begrudging those evacuee surviviors any one bit o all the lovely treats planned for them? Poor wee souls, and to think having lost sisters, brothers, playmates to that watery grave, even so they're still smiling and in good heart."

Sandy looked up. "Uch, Mima. Are ye beratin me for things Ah havenae even said?"

Andrew sensing that another family row was in the offing, suddenly said: "Mammy, see the day the survivors is goin tae the City Chambers, can Ah go alang tae George Square, just tae gie them a welcome-back cheer?"

Mima frowned. "Well ... noo ... Ah don't really know so much aboot that, son. Don't forget, the half o Glasgow will be there, tae see the brave wee souls in their new Scottish Highland outfits. One way and another, it'll be busier than any Fair Friday and we all know what that's like, wi drunks aff their heids wi the booze, and ither daft eejits all reelin aboot. No, son, mibbe best stay safe here at hame that day."

No sooner had she finished speaking, than Sandy exploded.

"For heavens sake, Mima, are ye really hellbent on makin a right nambie-pambie Mother's boy pansy oota oor son? We've had words aboot this before, ye cannae wrap the laddie up in cotton-wool for ever, it's jist no right, and Ah'll no be a party tae it a meenit longer."

Mima could feel the hot colour of anger rush to her cheeks, but even so her husband had not yet finished his tirade.

"God Almighty, woman, dae ye not see it ... these evacuee children are nothing short of heroes, torpedoed not once, but twice and lived tae tell the tale; heroes, bloody war heroes, that's what they are. And yet here ye are sayin it's no safe for oor son, even older than some of them, no safe enough for him tae venture far enough frae yer apron strings tae cheer them on their way and mibbe even wave a wee Scottish flag and gie a heartwarming cheer? Ah jist don't believe this."

Andrew grinned his delight and appreciation of his normally douce, don't-get-me-involved Father especially when the latter said: "Face it, woman what in God's name could possibly happen tae yer precious son between the Gorbals Cross and George Square? It's no exactly as if he's goin pioneering tae Timbuktu or nuthin, noo is it? And another thing ..." Sandy paused to draw breath, "If Andrew cannae achieve his ambition tae get tae Canada, at least have the decency tae let him go and cheer on those brave wee souls, brave enough tae keep on tryin against such odds. No too much tae ask, is it?"

Andrew piped in to say: "Uch, Ah might as well forget the whole idea of goin tae see them going intae the City Chambers, it's no even as if Ah have a flag, Scottish or ony other variety."

The longing in his voice pulled at Mima's heartstrings and by now in an agony of indecision, she rolled, unrolled then again rolled up a corner of the tea towel she held in her hands. "Andrew, ye know, if it was jist a flag we were talkin aboot …"

Granny's voice , feeble yet somehow rather more determined than of late, called over, "Andrew, Ah cannae think why ye'll no be allowed a wee bit flag for tae wave at the King and Queen when they're at Bellahouston."

As Andrew opened his mouth, about to correct his Granny as to her understanding of which particular event they were then discussing, his Mother put a warning finger to her lips and this together with a meaningful look was enough to silence him.

Mima then called over: "Aye, all right, Mammy, Ah suppose therr's nae real harm in lettin Andrew go along tae join in all the excitement on the big day, so thanks for that, Ma, and jist ye get back tae sleep, dear. Ye must be tired, ye'd a pretty restless time of it last night."

Then turning to her husband and son, Mima said: "Uch between the lot of youse, Ah seem tae be in the minority, so one way and another, it might be a good thing but even so ..."

As her halting words trailed away, the final decision was taken from her when her man, in a voice totally unlike his normally douce tones, said: "As ye know, Mima, and know well, it's no very often that Ah come the heavy Father, nae Victorian tyrant me, and it's no that often that Ah actually lay doon the letter of the law. But on this occasion, this momentous, aye, Ah'd even call it, this historic occasion, what Ah say, goes."

Mima and Andrew nodded silently in unison before muttering something about going to tell his pal Eck the good news, Andrew rushed from the room in a flurry of excitement.

TWENTY TWO

The untimely death of their beloved only son in a road accident in the thronged-to-capacity city streets was the stuff of nightmares. And while well-meaning friends and neighbours mumbled on that their hurt and grief would lessen with the passage of time, Mima, Sandy and even poor wandered Granny knew better. With each day that came and went, the chasm between the three of them deepened and became ever more damaging to their previously happy, contented home life. Normally talkative, Mima was aware that she had become withdrawn and silent ... terrified to say anything at all lest she end by verbally attacking her husband for his part in the tragedy. He it was, who, despite her own avowed objections, had decreed that her precious son could not possibly come to any harm in walking from Gorbals Cross to join the crowds gathered outside the City Chambers in George Square. Had she been strong enough to demand that he stayed safely at home then none of this need ever have happened .

If only ... if only ... if only.

Sandy too seemed to have taken something of a vow of silence in that with every minute of every day, he blamed himself. Even worse he knew beyond the shadow of a doubt that Mima blamed him and would go on blaming him for the rest of their lives.

Silence is golden, thought Mima. *Not in this house, not any more.*

The one and only sound, apart from the chimes of their wedding clock, the clatter of a spent coal as it hit the ashcan, was the occasional whining cry from the direction of the wallbed, when startled into wakefulness, her Mother would start weeping and say time and time again: "Where's Andrew? High time he was back from waving at the King and Queen. Ah wish he was home. He always sits and has a wee bit blether wi me every night before Ah fall asleep. Dae ye think he'll be very long now, Mima?"

Mima put a hand to her mouth to stem her own cry of despair ... *Is there tae be nae end tae this nightmare? Silence indeed. Hmph, complete silence might be golden, certainly would be preferable to this Greek chorus of ma Mother's.*

Mima sat down at the table and put her head in her hands. *Getting home, Mother, oh ma wee Andrew's home all right ... catapulted head-first intae his heavenly home. But how in the name of God can Ah ever hope to explain that to ma poor old Mother? By now, she's livin in a world of her own. And as for her not wantin anything new to upset her life, if it once dawned on her that her beloved grandson is not ever coming back ... why the shock of that would kill her. As the doctor told me, she's not harming anyone, so let her be. No harm in that way of coping with things.*

It hardly seemed possible that a year had gone by since the tragic death of their beloved only son. Even more amazing was the fact that through the entire year of grieving, as yet, they had managed to keep from Granny the real horror of the situation that her darling grandson would not ever be coming back.

There were days when Mima felt that with her emotions raw and always to the forefront of her very being, she knew she was being pushed to the very limit of human endurance.

Today, the anniversary of Andrew's death, when her husband for once spoke, it was not to bestow a kind or comforting word on her, but rather to bemoan: "Here Ah am a helpless cripple left to drag out the rest of ma days on this bloody earth while there's ma perfectly healthy young son sent poste-haste into Eternity."

At such times and from bitter experience, Mima knew better than to stroke his head and murmur would-be pacifiers. Instead and rather than try to argue or help him towards any possible understanding of such a dire situation, she would say: "He was ma son too, ye know."

His usual response was a twisting of his mouth and the words: "Can ye make any sense of a so-called loving God arranging such a calamity in our lives? Surely it would have made a helluva lot more sense to have taken me to his heavenly paradise and left our fine lad to grow to manhood. Before ye start quoting the Guid Book tae me, just save yer breath. Ask yer ain Mother over there snoozin peacefully in her bed, is it any wonder that she gave up on religion after the life she's had and even at that, she still disnae know a thing aboot what happened tae Andrew."

Mima could feel something snap in her mind and losing all reasonable thought, she at once marched over to her Mother, shook the old woman wide awake and yelled: "Right, Mammy, Sandy doesnae think ye should be spared the sad news a minute longer. He thinks ye've been shielded from reality long enough, he wants ye tae know ... now listen carefully for Ah'm gonnae say this only the once ..."

Her Mother, struggled up in bed as best she could and her eyes wide with the expectancy of hope she said: "It's Andrew, he's home, home for his tea at last, that's it."

Mima gulped, already regretting her impetuous action and she struggled to go on, but having come this far, she knew the time was right to inform her Mother of what must now be told.

"Mammy, it's bad news, really bad news, Andrew is no coming back home, never again ...ye see, he's dead, died in a terrible road accident. He's dead dae ye understand, dead."

The words had scarcely faded away when Bridget, gasped, fell back on her pillows and holding a withered hand to her chest she mouthed the word, dead. As her body sagged, a strange croaky sound came from her throat and Mima at once said: "Hold on, Mammy, Ah'll go for the Priest."

But even as she spoke, she knew it was already too late, she had failed to grant her Mother the only thing she had ever really asked of her. Mima's body shook with tears, as she sobbed her heart out with anguish, sorrow, guilt, but above all, guilt.

Somehow Granny's death seemed to help heal the breach between Mima and Sandy. In the months following, they gradually fell back into their previous comfortable relationship.

TWENTY THREE

September 1943

"Remember how the day war was declared the King in his broadcast tae the Empire said the nation should commit its cause to God?" Sandy said as they sat for a late cup of tea before bed.

"Aye, so …?"

"Just one thing bothers me … if they Jerries are sendin up prayers for their deliverance, how is the Man Upstairs supposed tae decide which one nation to save? Jist answer me that if ye can."

Mima gave a short laugh. "Listen, Sandy Ah'm far too knackered after ma late shift at that munitions factory to have any energy to spare for theological discussion, but Ah will say … some higher power must surely have been lookin after Hitler's Deputy. Bailed oot wi a parachute from his Messerschmitt 110 – when, away back in 1941? – and got away wi nuthin worse than a broken ankle when he landed in Scotland."

Sandy nodded. "Aye, Ah still remember the banner headlines in ma newspaper, 'Nazi leader flies to Scotland. Rudolf Hess in Glasgow Hospital'. Higher power be damned, what good did it dae poor Andrew, or me when Ah catapulted over a bit of stretched rope?"

Set in Her Ways

Mima shrugged. "Everything aboot this entire war set-up is weird, if ye ask me. and nobody knows that better than us, jist look how in four short years, it has transformed our lives. Me in a factory and ye running the phone for the Fire Watchers."

He gave her an appraising look. "As far as ma war effort wi the phones is concerned it all started yon time jist after yer Mother died and they started calling up older men and ye very kindly telt me that Ah'd be safe enough as it was only able-bodied men they wanted. That really hurt me, ye know, but it least it goaded me intae action, that's when Ah determined that Ah'd get aff ma bum and somehow dae ma ain bit for the war effort."

"Uch Sandy, ye've nae call for tae remind me of that terrible night. Ah could have bit oot ma tongue the minute Ah said yon awful things tae ye."

He nodded. "Well, it's all water under the bridge noo but Ah'll never forget after that row we had, when the next morning, ye didnae even hae the heart tae waken me as usual with yer normal rallying cry, 'Right, Sandy, that's yer porridge on the table.'"

Mima nodded. "Talk aboot biting aff ma nose tae spite ma face. Ah gret bitter salt tears all the way in the cold of the morning as Ah made ma way tae another day's cleaning, dusting and scrubbing. Never forget it, Ah should never have said yon cruel words tae ye, Sandy."

Next day, having made her peace yet again with Sandy, as Mima went off to do an extra nightshift at the munitions factory, she met up with Lizzie one of her work companions. As they walked along the streets in silence, suddenly Lizzie chuckled.

"Aye ye can say whit ye like aboot this war, but it's did a helluva lot o good for the likes of us, eh no?"

Unable to see her friend's face in the inky darkness of the street and ever mindful not of Hitler's bombs, but rather of the baffle-walls in front of communal closes, Mima kept her eyes downcast and said: "Funny ye should say that, Lizzie, for Sandy and me we were jist on aboot the very same thing the past few days. And although, when ye think of all the people being killed, it is a terrible thing tae say, even so, the war has certainly done us a power of good already, changed oor lives for the better."

Lizzie laughed. "Although Ah can see what ye're driving at, hen, mind ye, it wouldnae be everybody's cup o tea ... livin like ye and Sandy now dae, in the back-shop of the funeral parlour."

At once on the defensive, Mima said: "It's all tae dae with Sandy's war effort, if ye must know, him manning the telephone set-up in the back and of course, keepin the place open in readiness for the fire-fighters, the Home Guard wi their stirrup pumps and all their orders. That's why we're livin there."

"Aye, so ye tell me, but did youse really have tae upsticks oota yer single-end and go and live in a bloody funeral parlour? Ah mean tae say."

Already tiring of the conversation, Mima said: "It's a real cosy wee but-n-ben and anyway, it's no all doom and gloom. Sandy telt me they'd a rerr laugh the other night ... wee Billy Moore brought down a poke of pieces for his Paw and whit does the wean dae? ... only bung them doon on a nearby coffin"

Lizzie gasped. "Oh my. But Ah cannae see anything even remotely funny aboot that, Ah must say."

Mima laughed. "One of the firefighters says: 'Haud on therr, sonnie, show a bit of respect.' Well, the wean can see they're all sitting roon a coffin playing a game of cards, so he wonders whit's the difference, a packet of playing cards or a packet of Spam sandwiches? So that's when Sandy tells the wean, 'Aye, sonnie, but that one in the corner, it's occupied.'"

As the two women laughed, Lizzie said: "Helluva good that, and if they were in danger of dying of laughter, they were in the right place, eh no? Mind ye, ye couldnae make it up, could ye? Tell ye somethin else that's bloody daft ... see these baffle walls ... Hitler hissel couldnae hae built a better weapon, crashin intae them in the blackout, the half o Glesga's been knocked stupit. Neither use nor ornament."

"Talkin of which, better keep yer eyes on the lookout, or we'll be the next victims."

Lizzie said: "Thanks for the warning, Mima. And Ah'll tell ye sumthin else, see yon Wilma Strang ... she's aye been a battered wife since the hour and day she merrit yon big Tommy of hers. But noo, whit does she dae? Only blames every black eye, swollen jaw and bruised arms and legs on the baffle-walls. Pure deid convenient, that."

TWENTY FOUR

The war which had decimated the lives of many thousands of innocent people was now over. The back shop of the funeral parlour was no longer the nerve centre for the local air-raid wardens but had reverted to its normal peacetime use and Mima and Sandy were yet again living in a single-end, this time an even pokier one round in Mathieson Street. That morning on her way round to her latest wee cleaning job in Scotland Street School, Mima groaned inwardly as she spotted the approach of old Mrs Harris.

Old, thought Mima. *She's no older than me, but it's the way she goes on and on about her many real or imagined ailments ye'd think she was ninety at least and heading at high speed doon the brae towards the graveyard.*

Too late now to dart into any convenient close, Mima was suddenly aware of a hand on her arm and a petulant voice saying: "Wait 'til Ah tell ye the latest ... ma doctor's real worried aboot me, fair puzzled he is and ..."

By now fully aware that Moanin Minnie was determined to describe in graphic detail every last one of her symptoms, Mima hurriedly freed her arm and said: "Uch, it's yerself , Mrs Harris, sorry, hen, but Ah cannae stop, Ah'm late areddies for ma wee job."

Mrs Harris, not in the least put out, "Ye're far too conscientious, Mima MacRae. It didnae dae ye ower much good at yon Picture Hoose, noo did it, years of hard work and devotion, all for sweet bugger-all at the end?"

Refusing to be drawn into a discussion about a subject which still rankled with her, Mima took a step away.

Seeing this evasive action, but in a last ditch attempt for a captive audience, Moanin Minnie again grabbed Mima's arm.

"Ah thocht ye'd hae been interested tae hear aboot what ma doctor said tae me, him never have seen the likes of ma condition in all his years as a medical doctor, but if ye havenae got the time, at least just answer me the one thing, have ye had yer letter?"

Mima frowned. "Letter? Who'd be sending me a letter? Mind ye, yon nice wee postie, the one that got the gaol, he used tae take pity on lonely old souls that nobody ever cared tuppence aboot and jist give them a bundle of any letters from his bag, jist oota the goodness of his heart and tae make them think that somebody loved them."

Mrs Harris, rather than enjoying the opt-repeated tale of their locally admired latter-day Robin Hood, gave a sour look. "Oh him. Nae bloomin wonder they shoved him intae Barlinnie, a damned heid-banger, yon eejit. Ma man used tae cry him Shirley Temple what wi his curly hair stickin oota his uniform bunnet and the daft way he kinda danced in and oot the closes, scatterin the mail like confetti ... that's tae say, the letters that he hadnae already drapped intae the nearest puddles."

Mima laughed. "A real character, ye've certainly got that right, cheered us up, as if he was scattering sunbeams, But lissen, Ah'm wasting time, what was it ye said? Ye mentioned a letter for me, what's that all aboot?"

Mrs Harris folded her arms across her ample girth. "It's no jist for ye, we're all gettin them ... they're gonnae demolish oor tenements and we're all tae be rehoused."

Mima gasped. "That cannae be right, these buildings, they'd last another hundred years, built tae last so they are."

But Moanin Minnie, pleased to have been the harbinger of bad news nodded her head sagely. "Ah'm just tellin what's in the letters, the way it's gonnae be and there's damn all the likes of us can dae aboot it."

Refusing to be drawn into a futile debate, Mima said: "Tell ye one thing, hen, if Ah don't get a move on right now, Ah'll be jobless as well as homeless, and Ah wonder what ma man would say to that, for now that the war's over, times is as hard as ever before. Ah was earnin good money at yon munitions factory. Anyway, hen, cheerio for

the now ... and good luck at the doctor's.
Cheerio."

TWENTY FIVE

Ever since, long years after the war, they had been decanted into a high-rise flat, Sandy had felt like the King of the Castle. With his wheelchair and the nearby lift, he enjoyed the extra freedom and many a wee trip to Glasgow Green he was now able to take on the good days. At these times, wallowing in such independence, he'd say: "No, Ah'll be fine on ma own , hen Ah'll meet some of ma pals at the Old Men's Hut. So jist ye sit back and enjoy this lovely flat, look at the view. Ah'm sure that's the Campsie Hills we can see, marvellous, intit?"

But no sooner would he be out of the flat than Mima would start to worry about him – *Would he get back safe, would the lift, a bit wonky at the best of times, would the lift still be working all right? And if it really did break down altogether, how in God's name could she ever possibly get Sandy and his wheelchair back up the fifteen flights of stairs?*

As she made herself a cup of tea, she knew, of course, from which dark memory arose such gloomy, unnerving thoughts. *Danger did lurk in the streets of Glasgow, didn't it? Her poor innocent wee boy had found that.* Unwilling to follow that line of thought, Mima then turned to yet another worry and it was a secret she had shared with nobody, that ever-growing and now occasionally bleeding lump on her back.Mima pursed her lips. "Uch tae hell with it all, a harmless lump, that's no real worry.What Ah really hate, cannae stand is this damned flat, all mod cons or not. No wonder Ah'm feeling depressed, somehow Ah feel trapped here, a bird in a gilded cage."

Ever since she had been a wee girl at Primary School in Scotland Street, when the other children were drawing castles, Mima had always been perfectly content to create on paper her usual wee cottage. How the notion, far less the mental image, had arisen in the first place, she had no idea. Her cottage was a long, low single-storey whitewashed building with a door in the middle and on each side a window overlooking a shimmering sea and a cloudless sky. Not only did the door have a brass lion's head, and gleaming letterbox, above the lintel a riot of roses such as she'd seen in the park, cascaded in a blaze of colour. This image was still fresh in her mind when having braved the uncertainties of the creaking lift, she arrived at the Pensioners' Lunch Club, just in time to meet up with her friend, Bella. Later over a cup of tea and a digestive biscuit to finish, Mima was dimly aware of her friend blethering on regardless.

"Mima., for the love of goodness, what on earth's wrong with ye today? Ah've hardly had a word out of ye this dinnertime. And ye know how much Ah look forward to ma Wednesdays, the only day Ah can get out of ma high-rise, providing the lift's working. It makes ma week so it does, getting out on a Wednesday and oor wee blether aboot old times. Ye know, Ah'm that terrified of yon lift, Ah don't even venture out tae Church now. Aye, the old days was better."

Mima swivelled her head. "Sorry, Bella, just got a lot on ma mind"

Bella bent forward. "Is it yer arthritis playing ye up again? Ah tell ye, it's the dampness in these bloody flats, if ye'll pardon ma French. Ah don't very often swear, but see those high-rise boxes, they'd make a saint swear, so they would. Give me the old tenements, they were the best, at least we had great wee coal fires, and windows ye could have a real good hing-oot o. Aye, we got plenty of fresh air in them days, eh no?"

Unaware of what a raw nerve she had just touched, Bella opened her mouth to continue speaking but Mima spoke first. Knowing that she was far from pleased at Bella's concern for her health, she snapped before she could stem the words: "Ah'm perfectly all right, thank ye. And Ah'll have ye know, ma arthritis ... no need for ye to worry, it's a lot better now that Ah take ma morning tot o cod liver oil and also since Ah started going to the Pensioners' Swimming Morning, Now, can we leave the subject?"

Bella drew back. "Nae need tae bite ma face aff. Anyway, glad tae hear that ye're in such tiptop condition, ye'll be entering the Gala next."

Already regretting her outburst, Mima said: "Sorry, Bella, there's jist times, especially when anybody mentions the old days, and the guid life we had in the tenements, it jist fair upsets me, for those days are long gone."

Bella patted her friend's hand. "Dinnae fash yersel, Mima, we're all the same on oor bad days. Anyway, talkin o swimming ... how dae ye fancy a Mystery Tour, Pensioners' Paddle doon the water? Mibbe we could put oor names doon for that, what dae ye think? Dae ye fancy a day at Largs, Dunoon, Rothesay? Or mibbe it'll be Saltcoats they'll take us tae."

TWENTY SIX

As the boat sailed into Rothesay Bay, the passengers were greeted with the skirl of the pipes and the uniformed Harbour Master at the foot of the gangway, on hand to help the less able among the Pensioners' Paddle Party. Also, the Assistant Harbour Master, Peter, was already jollying along the aged visitors and bringing a blush to many a withered cheek with such comments as: "Right then, girls, don't all rush at once, but Ah'll be yer lumber at the dancin the night. Hello there, darlin, and where have ye been all ma life?"

On hand also was a bus waiting pierside to take the pensioners for a wee run round the Island. Once on board, the chirpy bus driver announced that there was a complimentary wee poke of sweeties on each seat and that if they they'd try no tae choke on the soor plooms, then they could have a wee sing-song. This was greeted by cheers from those not already chomping their way through the contents of the sweetie-poke, and a few ragged attempts at singing, *The Day We Went Tae Rossy-oh*.

When it was announced that their tour of the lovely Island of Bute would culminate in a complimentary lunch at the Pavilion, courtesy of the Rotary Club of Rothesay, and the not too subtle hint that there might even be a miniature or two of good honest Scotch whisky as prizes for the best recitation or song, this got an even bigger cheer. As the bus pulled away from the pierside and headed out along the Ardbeg shore past Skeoch Wood towards Port Bannatyne, some of the men in the party who'd brought along wooden noisemakers, rattled them to great effect. Somebody else got going with a hastily-produced mouth organ, Bella tried her 'prentice hand at music making on a comb and tissue paper. Then with party streamers, and even balloons flying in the breeze from the open windows and waving from local people out shopping or walking along the promenade, suddenly the party was in full swing. Mima sucked happily at her soor ploom.

"Ah'll leave the music making in yer hands, Bella," she said. "Bella, thank goodness ye telt me aboot this outing, even though at the time we didnae know where we'd end up. It made it all the more exciting, didn't it, it being a mystery tour. But this is great."

Her friend smiled. "At least it's put ye in a better mood. And Ah suppose gettin a day off from looking after yer guid man, gives ye a wee break. Mind ye, it's a wonder that he didnae want tae come as weel, plenty o helpers. They could have manhandled his wheelchair nae bother, same as they've did already wi those other wheelchairs and zimmers."

Mima said nothing and Bella laying aside her musical comb, said in shocked tones: "Ah suppose ye did tell him aboot this trip?"

Mima could feel the hot colour rush to her cheeks. "Well, no in so many words. Of course Ah telt him Ah was going, but somehow from what Ah said or didnae say, he got the impression that there were nae seats left."

Bella giggled. "Mima, ye'll go tae the Bad Fire telling lies, did yer Mammy never tell ye that?"

To cover her guilty embarrassment, Mima suddenly pointed to the window. "Oh Bella, would ye look at that. Therr's ma ain wee seaside cottage, jist the way Ah've always imagined it."

Bella laughed. "Ah didnae know ye were a landowner. But listen if it's a cottage ye're after, we could put oor names down for yon riverside sheltered housing."

Mima shook her head. "Sandy would never agree, he likes his high-rise."

TWENTY SEVEN

1990

Mima MacRae sat on the edge of the chair and looked towards the doorway at frequent intervals. So far, and despite having been told that, 'the Doctor will be with you shortly' as yet no Doctor had appeared. Nor for that matter had anyone else and after all this time of tense uncertainty and what seemed like an eternity of waiting, Mrs MacRae was beginning to worry about something else. Between the cold weather and with her being 'in the nerves' she knew that any minute now she would need to leave this waiting room and go off with as much speed as she could manage in search of the nearest toilet. Even as this thought crystallized in her mind, she was all too aware that never having been in this hospital before, the geography of the place was foreign to her.

Come to think of it Ah've never been in any hospital, even Andrew was born, now close on sixty years ago. Sixty years? That can't be right. Let's see ... Ah think ...

Just as she was starting to do a spot of mental arithmetic, more than anything to take her mind off the urgency of her physical need, the door opened to admit a fresh-faced young man.

Set in Her Ways

Hmph, she thought, *probably he's some student lackey sent in to do somebody else's dirty work by telling me yet again in suitably calming and appealing tones that 'the Doctor will be with you shortly.'*

In total silence the two stared at each other like actors in an ill-rehearsed play, they were waiting for their cue. Then having hurriedly glanced at a sheet of paper in his hand, the young man now all beaming bonhomie said: "Hi there, Mima , I'm Doctor Dainsbury, but please, just call me Guy"

Mrs Mima Ernestina MacRae on hearing this looked at the young doctor in total amazement. And although she uttered not a single word in reply to his invitation, she did throw him a meaningful look over the top of her half-glasses.

Inwardly, she knew that a look delivered in such a way would most certainly not be lost on anyone of her generation. At the same time her gut feeling was that it was being totally wasted on this trendy, super-confident young doctor.

As she waited with pursed lips for him to go on with whatever it was he'd come into the room for, she thought: *Now, there is something else that's changed in today's world – no respect for anyone whatever their status in life. For him to breeze in here, call me Mima as if we'd been firm friends for years! And as for me calling any strange man – far less a Doctor by his first name the very minute Ah clapped eyes on him – as they say now on every possible occasion, forget it.*

She became aware that he was speaking to her as she again turned to face him, she was in time to hear him say: "Right then, Mima, I just want to jot down a few details, take a blood sample and then Bob's your uncle, we'll admit you to a reception ward upstairs. That okay with you?"

Mima nodded, somewhat bemused by now and fully aware that okay with her or not, the whole thing was by way of being a hypothetical question. Taking her mechanical nod as due acceptance of the outlined designated procedure he dragged along a plastic chair. Then sitting almost knee-to-knee with her, he went through the details of who she was, date of birth, address, marital status, when she'd first noticed the lump – all of which data he seemed to have already on his clipboard as he quite happily and with the greatest aplomb ticked his way down the list.

Then, formalities over it, was back again to: "Right, now then, Mima – just a wee pin prick. I can promise you won't feel a thing – a blood sample for the lab, then we're done."

True to his word, Mima had to agree that she had not felt a thing to which he beamed and said: "Good! Wasn't too bad after all. Righty-ho. Then, Mima, if you'll just wait here, somebody will be along shortly to collect you."

Mima could feel her face tighten with annoyance

Now he's making it sound as if Ah'm a sort of package to be collected from left-luggage. And another thing – just how shortly is shortly likely to be?

She took a deep breath and with the thought, *Well, it's now or never before there's an accident,* she said: "Doctor just one thing – it's er ... Ah'll have to pay a call, ... but please can ye tell me where is the nearest ... er ... the ..."

He rose to his feet. "No probs, dear lady, no probs, if it's the loo you're after – see that door over in the corner there? There's an ensuite loo there for the convenience of patients."

Mima had previously noticed the unmarked door, but not given to snooping, she hadn't even thought of investigating. Feeling annoyed for giving herself such untold misery all afternoon she thought: *Perhaps Ah am too hidebound in my attitude. Nowadays everybody seems to do their own thing without so much as a please, or by yer leave.*

Still feeling annoyed at her own stupidity and timidity, she watched as Dr. Guy Dainsbury started gathering up his clipboard, stethoscope and other bits-n-pieces. That done, as he looked over at her she gave him another of her special looks as she thought: *If he addresses me again by my first name, Ah'll give him a piece of my mind. Yes! Ah will.*

The young Doctor shook her hand.

"That's us all done and dusted. Take care, see you around, Mi ... er ..." another glance at his clipboard, "Mrs MacRae. Yes! Bye now ... er ... Mrs MacRae."

As Mima shuffled her way to the ensuite she had a quiet smile to herself.

So, now Ah'm to be called by my Sunday name – perhaps the dirty look wasn't lost on him after all. Although come to think of it, if first names are the order of the day and the way things are done these days, mibbe Ah should just forget the old days and try to get used to it. It could have been worse – he could have called me Granny. Mind ye, given the disparity in our ages, great-Granny would have been more accurate. But then – nowadays in this compensation culture, by calling me Granny, Ah could have regarded that as an infringement of ma human rights since Ah am not a grandmother and could well resent having such a sexist age-label appended to me.

As she sank down onto the toilet seat she thought: *Anyway, the important thing is –Thank God Ah had the courage eventually to broach with him the subject of the whereabouts of the nearest toilet ... Don't think Ah could have held out much longer.*

As she re-entered the waiting-room, Mima MacRae settled as comfortably as possible in the plastic chair and picking up a years-out-of-date magazine, she thought: *Now all that remains is for me to be collected.*

Later that day on first being admitted to the four-bed ward, Mima took a hurried and decidedly anxious look around. She breathed a sigh of relief.

Set in Her Ways

Thank ye, God – my prayers have been answered. This is not a mixed-sex ward and not a drug crazed drop-out druggie in sight either.

This past month, when she'd been told in no uncertain terms that inconvenient or not, a stay in hospital was inevitable, Mima had spent sleepless nights agonizing over the lurid newspaper accounts of wards where men and women were packed in together with not a thought for decency, propriety nor even a vestige of any one person's dignity. Even worse, her one person's dignity.

Her friend Annie at the Age Concern Centre had gone into graphic detail about the time she'd spent in a mixed ward when a mentally confused old man obviously still thinking himself the lothario of his youth, had crawled into her hospital bed in the middle of the night.

As Annie pointed out, in yet again, regaling her friends with this horrific tale: "My screams would have awakened the dead and if that old bastard had thought his years of paying his dues into the National Health Service entitled him to such extras, Ah bloody well soon put the old bugger right. Confused or not, he wishae that much away in the fairies – just a damned chancer, if ye ask me."

There often followed a general discussion after each telling of this oft relived event, the concensus of opinion being: "Ah hope to God Ah never end up in any mixed ward. Ah couldnae thole that. One thing's sure, nae politician's old widowed Mother or Granny would ever be bunged intae something like that."

"Aye – old story, one law for the rich and another for the likes of us."

All this was going through Mima's mind, together with the thought that not a day passed but what yet another newspaper account or in-depth television investigation reported that to add to the situation even out-of-their-minds 'druggies' were also part of the indiscriminate human mix in large hospital wards.

"Honestly, between: call-centres, press this button, press that, telephone banking, soul-less supermarkets, mobile phones, automatic cash dispensers, computers and all the rest – sometimes feel like Ah've just landed from another planet."

Unaware that she had voiced this latter sentiment, Mima was surprised when the white-haired lady in the next bed said: "Whit was that? Sorry, hen, but Ah'm a wee bit deaf – didnae quite catch whit ye said. Ah'm Mrs King by the way."

As Mima introduced herself, her neighbour at once launched into a full account of her own past operations, a detailed description of the food, and which consultants were that high and mighty, showing off to their posse of students, that ye felt ye were supposed to curtsey or at least clasp yer hands and bow yer head in prayer when they spoke.

With Mrs King still in full oratorical flow, her words eventually had the effect of lulling

Mima to sleep. When next morning she awoke, having enjoyed the best night's sleep she'd had in weeks, it was to the realization that her right arm was stiff, rather painful and somewhat dramatically bruised from wrist to elbow.

On pointing this out to the young nurse, the latter grinned and somewhat airily said: "Oh! not to worry, Mima, no probs, that would be our Guy – hasn't quite got the knack of it yet."

At the mention of his name, there was much girlish laughter and even ribald comments from the nurses and their aides, much of this repartee, the full meaning of which went over Mima's head.

But old toothless Mrs King, a wee bit deaf or not and obviously a seasoned client of this particular ward, she seemed to home in on the full savour of the suggestive innuendoes and was laughing every bit as heartily as the young nurses.

Then wiping the tears of laughter from her lined cheeks, she said: "See ye lassies, that's terrible, so it is, talking about a fine young Doctor like that. Give the lad his due – he took a blood sample from me last week and say what youse like – but Ah think he's getting better at stickin it in."

Shrieks of pseudo scandalized laughter from the nurses greeted this confirmation of young Dr. Dainsbury's abilities. The hilarity reached a level of near hysteria when in all innocence Mima remarked: "He told me, it wouldn't hurt a bit – just a wee pinprick, then it would be all over."

By now holding on to a bed-end for support, Nurse Tracey composed herself sufficiently to say: "Aye, Mima, the same lad has said that many a time – Nurse Keira, over there, she can vouch for that one."

As finally the laughter died away, Tracey grinned at Mima and her neighbour and said: "Who needs the telly when we've got you two comedians on the ward. Anyway, enough of this hilarity, there's work to be done. Consultant's round in an hour – better get our skates on."

Once the four patients had been topped and tailed, the beds smoothed over, the locker-tops cleared of everything pertaining to patients' comfort and with everything shipshape and not a bottle of Lucozade nor a packet or box of tissues in sight, Tracey then turned to the two women whose innocent repartee had caused such an uproar and said: "Now then, you two, Sarah and Mima, behave yourselves – Mister Weston stands for no nonsense."

When the Consultant and his team stopped at Mima's bed, Mr. Weston gave a curt nod, the only indication of a, "good morning", then without further ado, he outlined the procedure he had in mind. Speaking to his students rather than directly to the patient herself he said: "As already explained at last week's clinical consultation, I shall remove the tumour. We've already established it is malignant and then we'll see where we go from there. Again I would point out," –

here he glared at Mima, "you should have seen about this much earlier. This required urgent attention the moment it started bleeding."

Mima opened her mouth to explain something of her past home circumstance and also to reaffirm that while she would be taking the operation she had her own views as to whether or not to go the route of radio and/or chemo-therapy.

But the Consultant having had his say, had already moved away from her bedside – but not before Mima heard him say to his team: "Old story, I'm afraid – who cares for the carer?"

As she fell back against the pillows, she thought: *Well, he's certainly got that right. Let's hope he's as good a surgeon as he is a psychiatrist. For Ah'll need to get well to look after my Sandy.*

TWENTY EIGHT

As Mima slowly emerged from the primeval mists of anaesthesia it was to the realization that 85 years old and having just had a cancer op or not, she was still in the land of the living. And in the strange new world of the 1990s, the person sitting at her bedside was none other than her 'named nurse'.

Aye, she thought, *nowadays this compulsion, fascination with names – changing the titles of businesses here, there, right, left and centre – and why a 'named nurse' of all things – doesn't everybody have a name without all this performance?"*

As Mima became aware that the woman was speaking to her, she tried hard to focus – *what nonsense was this – of course, Ah'm not a widow. That's why Ah have to get better as soon as possible – to look after my Sandy.*

Again the woman's words broke into her thoughts, as having consulted the inevitable clipboard – Does everybody clutch a clipboard these days? – the named nurse said: "It says here in your notes that you've been a widow for the last two years, and that your current address is Tower Court."

Mima tutted.

"Hmph! Tower Court – indeed a right fancy name for a high-rise with me on the 15th floor, no less – lifts always breaking down – they shoved me into that when they demolished my old tenement – a far better house than Tower Court could ever be".

Chelsea reached forward and patted Mima's hand. "There now, don't you go upsetting yourself dear – we'll talk about this tomorrow. We are of the opinion that a Care Home would be a much more suitable environment for you."

Mima tried to raise her head from the pillow. "A Care Home – ye mean somebody's gonnae care for me?"

Another pat at her hand. "Yes, my dear and about time too. With your State Pension, it won't cost you a thing. So, just you get a wee snooze now."

As Chelsea still clutching her clipboard badge of office departed and Mima could feel herself again drifting off into the land of nod, her last thought was: *But Ah read in the papers, they make old folk sell their houses to pay for their care. But, Ah havenae got a bought house, so does that mean naebody will care for me. But Chelsea … she said something about my State Pension, did she no?*

These thoughts scrambled through her head until feeling herself drifting off into sleep again, Mima became aware of something else: *Oh! here, Ah cannae worry about that noo, there's more important matters than that … Ah can see my Sandy, he's waiting at a gate for me. Oh! Sandy, my lovely man — ye're better — ye're no a cripple anymore and Ah can feel yer arms around me. Oh! Sandy!*

EPILOGUE

Kelsey and Amanda, the two young social workers sent to sort out, evaluate the contents and then dispose of the rubbish from Mrs Mima MacRae's fifteenth storey Tower Court flat, got down to work straight away.

"Not like some of the dumps we're sent out to deal with, is it, Amanda?" The girl thus addressed nodded, grinned and said: "At least this particular dump is spotlessly clean and tidy. Mind you, not much of a place for an old lady in her eighties and certainly little in the way of creature comforts."

As Kelsey finished speaking, she looked up and said "It'll not take us long to complete this job, so tell you what – Amanda, suppose you take the bedroom and I'll do the kitchen. That way, we should finish in double-quick time and have time for a coffee before our next assignment."

They had each been working in their separate areas when suddenly, after about fifteen minutes or so, Amanda called out: "Kelsey! Can you come into the bedroom for a minute – something to show you."

The something turned out to be a fox fur, complete with staring eyes, tail and down hanging

151

claws. Amanda was holding the object aloft, yet at arm's length as she pointed out to her colleague "First time I've ever seen one of these at close quarters – but old pictures of my two Grannies – they used to wear things like this."

Kelsey laughed and gave a mock shiver of repulsion "Enough to give you the creeps, the very idea of draping a dead fox around your neck. Some fashion that was, I don't think." Her friend nodded and said: "I think we're agreed – that's one item for the rubbish bin – not even charity shops will accept furs of any kind – anyone who'd be seen dead wearing this – deserve to have a tin of paint thrown over them."

As the two young women giggled together, Kelsey pointed to a plastic bag she held in her hand "If you think that's weird, just wait 'til you see what I found in the kitchen." So saying she opened up the bag and held it out for inspection.

Amanda peered inside.

"A mouldy old loaf – nothing strange about that, surely?"

Without another word, Kelsey lifted out the loaf to reveal the cavity that had been carved into the middle of it and which appeared to hold a wedge of rolled-up bank notes. On closer examination this turned out to be a number of ten shilling notes and a large tissue paper fiver.

As the girls studied this secret hoard, Amanda was of the opinion: "I'm not sure that these old banknotes are still legal tender. Uch!, the poor old soul – probably had them under her bed for years, then made a safer hiding place for her treasure before she went into hospital."

The girls finished their task and went off to write up the necessary report. As they went back down in the creaking lift, Kelsey said: "When you think of it, poor soul at the end, she didnae have much tae show for a lifetime spent on planet earth did she?"

Amanda nodded. "Even if she'd had the sense tae spend that wee pile of money before decimalization on anything with a wee bit of style, at least she'd have got some enjoyment out of all her scrimping and saving."

As they went out into the street, the last word was left to Kelsey. "Uch, well, somebody must have loved her. Did you notice the photograph on her sideboard of her and a man with his arms round her with the caption, 'me and Sandy at Largs'."

Amanda laughed "Good old Sandy, whoever he was – not a bad looking man – her taste in men must have been better than her dress sense."

The End

Jenny Telfer Chaplin

Also by Jenny Telfer Chaplin:

The Candleriggs Trilogy
Beyond the Bridge of Time
A Life to Live in Glasgow

Available as Ebooks from www.Bewrite.net and through Amazon and Barnes& Noble

A Daughter is for Life

Available in print from www.Lulu.com and through Amazon and Barnes & Noble.